T0103528

My Darling

My Darling

DR. SATISH CHANDRA

PARTRIDGE
A Penguin Random House Company

Copyright © 2016 by Dr. Satish Chandra.

ISBN: Hardcover   978-1-4828-5812-9
               Softcover   978-1-4828-5811-2
               eBook   978-1-4828-5810-5

All rights reserved. No part of this book may be used or reproduced by any means, graphic, electronic, or mechanical, including photocopying, recording, taping or by any information storage retrieval system without the written permission of the author except in the case of brief quotations embodied in critical articles and reviews.

All the characters in this book are fictitious, and any resemblance to actual person, living or dead, is purely coincidental.

Because of the dynamic nature of the Internet, any web addresses or links contained in this book may have changed since publication and may no longer be valid. The views expressed in this work are solely those of the author and do not necessarily reflect the views of the publisher, and the publisher hereby disclaims any responsibility for them.

Print information available on the last page.

To order additional copies of this book, contact
Partridge India
000 800 10062 62
orders.india@partridgepublishing.com

www.partridgepublishing.com/india

This book is dedicated to my all friends

Prolog

Hey Enan, what're you looking at?

Sori, see that female.

Do you like or love her?

I don't know, but I'm getting attracted.

So, what's your plan?

I'll befriend her, maybe date her to know if she'll make a good girlfriend.

Okay, if you succeed, what next?

I'd like to live with her to know if she's the one.

Do you think live-in relation may offer you the best course to find your darling- a perfect partner?

Of course. Any doubt?

You're totally mistaken. There is no perfect person in this world. Better read "My Darling" to know what happens with people having live-in relations. Are they really happy married couple?

Have you read it?

Yeah. It's worth reading.

Where is the book?

Here is the book- "My Darling"; read it yourself to know how you can find your darling or make a good couple.

"My Darling"

Chanting of 'Chai-Chai' woke me up. I saw my watch, it was showing 5.30 a.m. It means train is right time and still there is an hour to reach Dehradun. I was going to Mussoorie to attend the alumni gathering and meet my old college friends, who're celebrating the Silver Jubilee of our graduation. The venue was fixed on request of Mr. Vinayak, who was in the hospitality business and owning a hotel in Mussoorie. The idea of meeting so many old friends was very exciting. There're sweet memories of old college days to share with. My parents used to say that student life is the best period of life, but I didn't agree with them at that time, considering studies as the most boring, troublesome and unpleasant thing one could ever have. I understood the true meaning of my parents' adage when I joined the service. In childhood, we'd had no botheration of life except to study and having fun with friends. One has no worry for earning his bread and butter or managing his domestic affairs. As one transits from the adolescence to adulthood and joins service, profession or business to earn his livelihood, he's confronted with all the hurdles of life. He's no time for fun that he used to love so much as a child. As a grown up and socially responsible person, he's busy in earning his livelihood or fulfilling his dream. When I told my son that student life is the best time one has, he uttered almost the same words, which I used to say to my father, 'Studies and exams are the most boring and unpleasant thing in life, you don't know the pain of studies.' My son sounded as if I've grown up without going to school and college. Now when I'm in the second half of my service career, it can be vouched that childhood is really a golden period of one's life. In childhood, one is free from the domestic burden and needs to just focus on his study and enjoy his life.

Marital adjustment is itself the biggest challenge of anyone's adult life, besides the struggle of earning bread and butter. The greatest irony of life is that unmarried people are busy in search of a perfect partner to marry and married souls curse their fate and time when they got married. We all know that man is a social animal and is distinguished from the rest of other species by his ability to speak and express his feelings, a unique quality which God hasn't gifted to other living creatures. However, unlike other species, human being got an amusing notion that God has created a perfect partner to complete him or her. In fact, male of all species chases female and vice-versa as a natural process of mating for procreation of living beings. It may be, perhaps, equally true for all other known and unknown creatures in this universe. Hence, search for a dream partner or a soul mate has been as old as the human existence and will continue to be so till this world exists. There's no one like a perfect partner or a perfect soul mate. That's why, the most famous Greek philosopher Plato had said that a perfect human being was tragically split in two, resulting in a race of creatures sentenced to spend the rest of their lives searching for that missing other part that can complete him. However, Hindu mythology presents 'Lord Shiva' as 'Ardh-nareshwar' a perfect union of male and female. This proves the issue of a perfect partner or soul mate had been the concern of people, belonging to different races and cultures from time immemorial, and may continue to be so in future also without any abatement.

My thought process got disturbed by a sudden jolt, I got with the jerky stoppage of the train. The co-passengers started getting ready to get off the train. It means we'd reached

Dehradun and I needed to get my luggage together. I got up hurriedly. I put on my shoes and collected my belongings quickly. I was still feeling very sleepy, but as I got off the train, a blow of cool breeze braced me up. I started looking out for the gentleman, who was supposed to receive me at the station. It didn't take me a long time and effort to spot the person with a placard of my name. I beckoned him. It was Mr. Mohan, who'd come to receive me. He appeared to be a very pleasant man with a smiling face. He welcomed me with a small bouquet and a big smile. He'd already arranged a coolie to carry my luggage. We waded through a big human stream, formed by the passengers, to the exit gate. The scene at the railway station was a usual one, except for the blow of fresh breeze, which is normally missing at the other railway stations of metropolitans and big cities.

As we stepped out of the platform and reached at the porch of Dehradun station, Mr. Mohan called the driver-Ramdeen, who came rushing. Ramdeen guided us to the car, parked in front of the exit gate. He adjusted my luggage in the boot of Innova, which appeared to be a comfortable vehicle for the journey from Dehradun to Mussoorie, a hilly terrain. Mr. Mohan advised Ramdeen to purchase a water bottle.

'Please buy a newspaper as well', I requested Ramdeen.

'Yes, sir', said Ramdeen and went to the nearby shop.

'Sir, is it your first visit to Mussoorie or have you visited this place earlier also?' Asked Mr. Mohan.

'I came to Dehradun for the first time about twenty years back to attend a 'Foundation Course' in the Mussoorie Academy and after that visited this city quite a few times. Today, I've come here after ten years,' I said to inform Mohan, who became more humble on getting this information and bending a little, said, 'Sir, you'll be staying in Hill top Hotel, located at ten minutes' walk from the Library point.'

'I think the city must have changed since my last visit,' I enquired.

'Definitely, Sir. You may observe that things have changed a lot after the formation of Uttrakhand- as a new state and Dehradun becoming its Capital. The city has witnessed huge constructions along with Rajpura road, leading to Mussoorie, which used to be dotted with green trees twenty years back,' said Mohan.

Ramdeen came back with a water bottle and a newspaper. Mohan requested me to board the car. We all boarded the car immediately and left for Mussoorie. Ramdeen appeared to be a good driver. He was focused on his work. As we drove through the city and set on the way to Mussoorie, it was apparent that the city became very congested over the period of time since my first visit. There was hardly any empty space left along with the road.

'Sir, would you like to visit Sahastradhara or go straight to Mussoorie?' Asked Mohan.

'Straight to Mussoorie', was my crisp answer. I was a bit restless to reach Mussoorie. I was really thrilled to meet my old friends for reviving our old memories.

It was a very pleasant morning. I'd kept my side car window opened to get cool breeze, which was really very refreshing. But somehow, I slipped into the lane of my memory to find myself in an old State Roadways bus, during my first visit to Mussoorie. It was a Tata Bus, filled with a strong stench of diesel. It rattled through the hilly road, emitting black smoke and making me puke frequently. That journey was really a nightmare and I can't forget it ever in my life. When I reached Mussoorie, I was totally exhausted. Somehow, I managed reporting to the Academy. It was a horrifying journey. The very same night, I suffered from fever and hill-diarrhoea. I'd a terrible time, because medicine didn't work. Somehow, after passage of three-four days, medicine responded and I felt relieved from the suffering. I regained my senses to know what was happening around me. The place was full of young, energetic and vibrant people, who're students till a day before. And now became responsible officers of prestigious Indian Civil Services. All're having their own dreams and aspirations in life. However, one thing was common among them- most of them were unmarried and in search of their dream partners or soul mates. Everyone wanted to marry a perfect girl or guy, as the case may be, but had different perceptions of a perfect partner. Good looking, tall and slim, fair skinned, rich family, status, political connections, good behavior, caring, housewife or working partner, cooking expertise, outgoing, dancer, knowledge of club etiquettes, singer, music lover, prospects of fat dowry were some expected attributes of a perfect partner as per the prospective soulmate hunters. Hardly a few understood- who was a good partner? I think most of them, including me, hoped to get a dream partner, who should've all the attributes, they desire. Though, they themselves have not had even half of their expected qualities. One of the reasons for such unreasonable expectation among Indian youth can be attributed to Bollywood factor. Movies have tremendous influence on Indian youth in shaping their impression about their soul mate. Most of the college going youth think, they're destined to meet their darling on the very first day of college-admission. Similarly, every girl dreams to find her charming prince, riding on a horse, to marry her someday. I wasn't an exception. First, I got fascinated with my neighbour, living at the entrance of the street I used to pass through to reach my housing complex. She was a slim, fair, intelligent and good looking girl from a middle class family. We used to chat occasionally, but never became good friends. There was some romantic inclination towards another friend, who wasn't very pretty and fair but sweet in nature. Somehow, we couldn't find enough common ground to stick together, leaving enough scope to remain in search of a perfect partner.

My mother was keen to have a caring housewife for her dear son, who was interested in marrying a working girl. I joined the Academy with this background. All my hopes to find a soul mate got shattered in a few days. I realised that each lady officer was having some or other qualities I was looking for, but none was having enough magnet to attract. Rima was very pretty but too liberal to befriend any boy. Laura, Sonia, Rumi, all're intelligent and beautiful, but they're certainly bereft of attributes required for raising a family. They can beat any macho-man in a boozing competition. Shalini was too simple and people used to call her 'Behenji (sister)'. This didn't mean no one could succeed in getting his or her dream partner. It was rumoured that about thirty four officers, out of more than three hundred trainees, could get their darling-prince/princess to enter into wedlock. One officer fell in love with a staff assistant and became lunatic after her refusal to marry him. Once you like someone, you start liking everything about her. And her particular quality, you're attracted to, may incapacitate you to appreciate her true nature as a whole. Your brain refuses to accept any rationality, leaving things to so called destiny which can't be tested objectively.

'Sir Ji, would you like to have tea?' Suddenly Mohan asked me. And it shattered my day- dreaming and brought me back to the real-world.

'Thanks, let's keep on moving,' I said.

'Okay, Sir,' answered Mohan and asked Ramdeen to continue.

I started watching the scenic beauty of the great Himalayan range. It was really strange to notice that most of the water streams were totally dried up and tree leaves weren't as green as they used to be in the past. It was, perhaps, my elusion or the reality of the pollution effect. Lot of constructions had taken place along with the road as informed by Mr. Mohan. Things had really changed due to ever-growing demographic effect. By the time we reached the Library point, I realized that moving forward was really traumatic. The Library point had become a very crowded place. Somehow, we managed to reach the hotel. Mr. Mohan contacted the receptionist and informed him about my arrival. Since my room was already reserved, it didn't take much time to get hold of the keys to my room. The hotel attendant took my luggage and guided me to my room. I thanked Mr. Mohan for all his courtesy and assistance extended to me.

'I'll be obliged, if you could arrange a list of the participants with their room numbers,' I requested Mohan.

'Sure Sir, it'll be my pleasure. I'll request the manager to provide you a list,' said Mohan and left my room.

Once he left, I ordered for tea and then started unpacking my suit case. I was looking for my shaving kit.

'Trine-Trine,' sounded the doorbell and I rushed towards the door to check visitor, leaving my suite case half unpacked. I opened the door to see room attendant who was standing with a bunch of papers. He was a smart looking young man in his late twenties, dressed in a red uniform.

'Sir, this's the list of the participants that you asked for,' he spoke gently and handed over papers to me.

I took the papers and thanked him. Once he left, I closed the door and started glancing through the list. I was very pleased to see name of Mr. Rajan Gangotra. We used to call him 'Raj'. He was supposed to reach the hotel before me, but somehow he got delayed and was likely to reach any time. My other college friends, who're expected to arrive in Musoorie, were Sophia, Robert, Rocky and Deepika.

'Trine-Trine,' doorbell rang again. I opened the door. It was a service boy, who came to deliver the tea. He came inside the room. He put the tea-tray gently on the side table and left the room quietly. I took the newspaper and started glancing through it, while sipping the tea. Once I finished the tea, I again started unpacking my suit case to take out my shaving kit. In the next thirty minutes, I was ready to go for the breakfast. I checked my mobile and noticed there're four missed calls. It was on mute hence I couldn't hear any ringtone. Three calls were from my wife, who must've been keen to know my safe arrival at Mussoorie. I talked to her briefly and informed about my journey and stay arrangement. One call was from Raj. I talked to him and enquired about his likely arrival time.

'I may reach Mussoorie in half an hour, so wait for me to join you for breakfast,' said Raj and disconnected the phone.

I sat down on a relaxing chair and started musing over Raj's encounters with women in his college days. He was a six fit tall, fair but slightly bulky young man. He used to be an interesting guy. He was a typical orthodox and conservative person in his social demeanour, like many other middle class Indians. Raj, however, would love to present himself as a modern guy, while befriending women. He used to dilly- dally with his college girlfriends and had sort of live-in-relations with a few of them.

Once I asked him, 'Raj! Do you think, your behaviour with your girlfriends is morally correct?'

'My dear friend, I don't care about right or wrong. I follow a great saying "Everything is fair in love and war". If I don't spend time with these girls, how can I know who'd be suitable for me to marry. How can I marry a girl without knowing her intimately? Spending time or living with a girl is the best course to know her. She can also judge me. If we find each other compatible, we can marry,' said Raj.

'I think the physical closeness isn't the right criteria to find your love. The body chemistry creates a spark or love at first sight when you meet someone. And your closeness may blossom into a true love in due course of time. If there's no spark and you start spending time together, it may create some interest. But, that interest or liking may vanish in due course and your relations may start to deteriorate...'

'It means, you agree that closeness creates affinity,' said Raj, interrupting me.

'Bloody moron, I'm saying living together mayn't necessarily create true love between two people, if there's no spark between them in their first meeting. Sometime closeness may result in strong liking and may or mayn't metamorphose into a true love,' I said.

'I disagree with you. In my view physical intimacy does create affection and love between two individual, while offering an opportunity to judge your partner,' said Raj.

'If physical union creates love, what's the need to judge your partner? You need to judge someone, if you don't love or trust her,' I countered.

'You may say what you like, but I strongly feel that proximity helps you to know others,' Raj said.

'Proximity is fine, but going beyond it to have physical relation isn't correct. It may spoil your marriage, if you happen to marry someone other than your live-in partner,' I said.

'How can live-in relation spoil a marriage? Raj enquired.

'Raj you know, every guy in India wants to marry a virgin lady and I'm sure you won't be an exception…'

'So what?' He interrupted me.

'Let me complete first and then you say whatever you want to,' I told him curtly.

'Alright. Please continue with your sermon,' Raj said politely.

'In the last two years, you've broken your relationship with four girls and I guess you'd physical relations with one or two. One day, these girls may become the wife of someone. It may happen, you get one of such girl as your wife; who had live- in- relation with someone and gets married with you after breaking her relationship. I'm sure, you aren't impervious to all such possibilities…'

'I know." Raj said, interrupting me. 'Let me enjoy my life. You're jealous of me and that's why you're talking all bullshit.'

'My dear friend, I'm saying all this as I care for you,' I said. 'And you think, I feel jealous of you. Remember my words- you may spoil your life. Your subconscious mind, having a lurking doubt about the virginity of girls, may refuse to trust your wife. Such distrust may always haunt your marital relations and may probably break your marriage.'

'Do you think, I'm so stupid to distrust my wife?' Raj questioned me.

'I'm not saying you're so stupid. It's a normal human mentality. When you've intimate relations with numerous girls, you're bound to compare them with your spouse. Similarly, your dream girl may keep on weighing your traits with her ex-boyfriends. This may shake the very foundation of your healthy marital bonding,' I said to explain him the consequences of flirting and live-in relations.

'Please don't give me lecture. Let me live my life on my own terms. I don't want to spend my whole life eating only one pudding,' said Raj, while expressing his unhappiness to me.

'Okay. Don't be angry, it's a friendly concern, I shared with you. Certainly, you're a master of your own destiny and nobody, except you, can change it. We'll see what happens in future,' I said and left him.

This was, perhaps, the last serious dialogue, I had had with him in the last year of college life. I joined a public sector company immediately after my graduation in law. And, both of us joined the Indian Civil Services, a year later. In the training, he got infatuated with one of the lady colleagues. He broke his relations with her after spending some time and got married with someone else, whose parents were settled in UK. He'd a frustrated family life, but a successful career. My meditative mood got disturbed with the sound of the doorbell. I got up to open the door. I saw, it was room service.

'Sir, can I clean the room?' He asked.

'No, thanks. It's already well attended,' I said and closed the door.

It was 10 a.m. when I got a phone call from Raj to know that he'd reported to the reception and might take ten-fifteen minutes to reach my room.

I switched on the TV and started flicking through channels. There was hardly any good programme, so I switched it off and started reading a newspaper. There was a small reporting in the local newspaper about our Alumni Meet. This puts me again in a brooding mood to ponder over another friend Sophia, who'd gone to the USA for her higher studies after completing her graduation in India. Sophia belonged to a rich family having sort of an international background. Sophia was very outspoken and bold in expressing her feelings. In those days, she was considered an ultra-modern lady. If one compares her with today's standard, she may be rated as a modest smart woman with western values. She was very proud of herself. She may compromise on anything, but certainly not on her self-respect. I met Sophia after twenty years, since she left the country. Our encounter was sudden and incidental. I'd gone to attend a wedding party, where I met her.

'Oh! Sophia. It's you, I can't believe it. Never expected you to meet at this marriage party. Let me pinch myself to ensure I'm not dreaming…'

'Jai! You haven't changed a bit, still keep on pulling my leg,' she said, while interrupting me. 'I left the country more than twenty years back to save myself from your punches, but, even after passage of such a long time, you're still maintaining your mischievous smile and naughty gestures…'

'Don't blame me for all this, it's just a reflection of your personality. I can't help myself. So, it's sure, I'm meeting my old Sophia darling and none else,' I said, while holding her hand.

'Yes and no,' said Sophia.

'What does it mean?' I asked her immediately without allowing her to say anything.

'If you allow me to speak, I can explain you,' she said.

'Please go ahead,' I said apologetically.

'Come on! Let's have something to drink and sit somewhere, so that we can chat comfortably,' she said and held my hand to take me towards the waiter serving the drinks. We took our drinks and sat down on a corner sofa. She started narrating her story.

'You know, I joined Boston University. There, I befriended one Mr. Jayant Subramaniaum, in short 'Subbu'. He hailed from the state of Tamil Nadu in India. He was very intelligent and good looking, smart man. He attracted me and we became buddies in a short span of time. We started hanging out. One day, we're just chatting, sitting in a park. Suddenly, he got up and plucked a flower. He then kneeled down on the ground in front of me and proposed, 'Can I ask this beautiful lady to marry me?' while offering me the same flower.

'Honey, you sound very romantic,' I said, while taking the flower from his hand. 'What's the matter, suddenly you became so romantic?' I asked him with a bit of curiosity.

'You're looking so hot today, I can't resist myself. I really want you to marry me before someone else takes you away,' he said with a big smile on his face and pulled me close to him.

First, I thought, he was jesting. 'Why are you tricking me? Didn't you get any one from the morning to tease?' I said and pulled my hand from his clutches.

'I mean so. I'm not trying to blink you. I'm not going to leave you till you give me your vow,' he said and again pulled myself closed to him. He paused for a moment and kissed me. I didn't resist this time. Having known him for some time, I accepted his proposal without any hesitation. We decided to get engaged formally during his parents' ensuing visit to Boston in the coming summer.

We started living together without waiting for our parents' approval and formal engagement. After spending a month's time with him, I realised he was a very conservative and orthodox Indian unlike his appearance. He was physically in Boston and mentally still in India. Living with him, I felt, I was in some south Indian home and not in the USA. He used to get up early in the morning and perform Puja before starting his day. He wouldn't speak to me, till he was finished with his daily rituals. It gave me an impression that he'd more faith in rituals than in God. He strongly valued male superiority and considered women a commodity to be possessed. He started treating me like a domestic servant rather than a friend. He expected me to cook and clean all the utensils alone rather than sharing the work with me. I felt, I was treated as a domestic helper rather than a friend. I was hardly getting time to concentrate on my study. I found him irrational and uncompromising in some matters. One day, I asked him, 'Subbu! Please tell me why don't you eat anything during solar or moon eclipse? I don't see any reason in keeping fast during an eclipse.'

He got irritated and said, 'What bullshit you're talking: are you ignorant? You're a Hindu lady and you don't know why Hindus in India don't eat anything during solar-eclipse. You should know, people pray to save Sun-God from the sufferings of Rahu-Ketu (Dragon-Stars).'

'Which God do they pray to save Sun? Sun is also considered a God, and that's why, you worship the Sun every day,' I questioned him.

'I haven't thought about it. I've been told by my parents to fast during eclipse, so I'd been fasting all through my life during an eclipse,' he explained.

'You're a physics student and know very well that an eclipse is a pure function of natural phenomena and has nothing to do with the sufferings of the Sun. Such beliefs are the result of superstitions and nothing else. Can't you apply the knowledge, you've acquired through your studies, in your day to day life,' I said, while challenging him.

'You're making fun of me. You're insulting me,' he said furiously to express his anger. 'You women have no brain and that's why women are prohibited from studying Vedas and performing many rituals...'

I strongly retaliated. And, while interrupting him, I said, 'Men were aware about women's competency and capabilities, that's why Vedic People used to worship women as "Shakti" (Power). People, like you, had deprived women of their right to study to enslave their labour and sexuality for satiating their lust.'

'You're questioning the wisdom of our ancestors, who prohibited females from reading scriptures. You think all Hindu scriptures are wrong?' He said without hiding his frustration.

'I didn't say all Hindu scriptures are wrong, but I don't believe in things blindly. Nothing in this world is infallible. Truth must pass the test of rationality. If you believe that all Hindu customs and practices contain the truth, they shouldn't sigh away to pass the litmus test of rationality,' I said all this in a very angry mood.

Having found himself helpless to defend his action, he left the room in a huff saying, 'I can't tolerate my insult. I don't think, we can go a long way.'

I cooled down and started introspecting to know what had actually gone wrong. I was under strong belief that I didn't say anything insulting or derogatory to him or to his religion, which wasn't his sole property and belongs to me equally. This incident forced me to re-evaluate our relations afresh. He could escalate such a small conversation to this extent, what may happen in future, if someday I really mess up, became my real concern. I left for my class in a disturbed mental condition. Since that day, our relations started deteriorating day by day and finally we separated instead of uniting.

A year down the lane, I met Richard- a German-American. He was teaching management at Boston University. We became very good friends and, since last fifteen years, we've been living together happily. We're in live-in-relation.' She informed me briefly about what had happened with her after leaving the college.

'Is Richard not interested in marrying you?' I asked, breaking the monologue.

'He's very keen to marry me. It's me, who always resist solemnising the marriage. I strongly believe, if we're in love with someone, we don't need external support of any institution to hold the bonding. The institution of marriage forces you to fake your relationship, even if you don't wish to stay together for a day. Had I got married with Subbu, perhaps, I might be still carrying the burden of so called a happy married life,' said Sophia to explain her point of view of having lived in relation rather than getting married.

'I don't agree with you. In my view, sex outside the marriage is a result of lust and infatuation. It may pretend to be a true love resulting from physical intimacy, but is nothing more than bodily exposure for sensual satisfaction. You may use the language of love and commitment, but it may be nothing of either...'

'How can you say so strongly?' Interrupting me she questioned. 'What do you know about love out of marriage? I can say with full confidence that I'm happier than any married person. We share our pain and pleasure together, like any married couple. We don't need to fake our relation. Had we not been in true love with each other, we could've parted long back. There's nothing which prevents us from separating, but we're staying together on our own volition.'

'If you consider your relationship with Richard as true love, please tell me why couldn't you accept the marital commitment? It's fictitious to suggest that true pleasure and intimacy can be had without loving and marital commitment. Live in relation by its nature suggests that partners have no intention to commit for greater responsibilities. They want to leave a window for escaping, from the so called love binding, at the very first available opportunity,' I said, while countering her point of view.

'You may not agree with me. I still hold my view tenaciously that Indian marriage institution obligates people to fake their happiness, despite the fact they may be living as a stranger under one roof. People aren't getting divorce easily because, even if someone want, the very legal system, his partner or family doesn't allow him to walk away. Whereas in a live in relation, if you don't love the person, you can easily walk out. I don't find the marriage institution relevant to my happiness, so I haven't opted for it,' she said emphatically to explain her views about marriage and live-in relations.

'You know very well the significance of a marriage and so have come to attend it from such a faraway place. All friends and relatives of the bride and groom are celebrating their future sexual relations, but no one will do so if the same couple opts for live-in relation. Similarly, all the friends and relatives may again rejoice pregnancy of the married lady, but they won't do so when an unmarried lady gets pregnant. Marital relations aren't just for physical pleasure, but to discharge a social obligation too. Whereas live-in relations or sex out of marriage is only meant for individual pleasure. Marriage provides stability and social respectability to relation as compared to live-in relations. Marriage prevents you from breaking relation in a fit of anger emanating from the loss of your mental equilibrium. I can vouch for it on my own experiences,' I said, while explaining my point of view.

'You think marriage gives some assurance and stability in relationships and prevent walking out on some small pretext. It may but, most of the time, it forces you to fake your relations. For example, had I got married with Subbu, I might've, perhaps, continued in wedlock without having any emotional attachment with him. This, I call faking of relationship. It's easy to abort such relation, if you aren't married,' she said very firmly, while betraying her distrust about marriage institution.

'I see your vantage point. There's an exception for everything. You may be experiencing true happiness in your live-in relation. And I'm happy in my married life. Human life is very complex, so can be a married life. Marriage will not be a panacea for all the problems. But, it's needed not only to regulate sexual human behaviour for sustenance of the society, but also to many other individual rights like property, succession, etc. You know people, having live-in relations, mostly don't have children. If everyone opts for a live-in relation, how can a society survive?' I said to challenge her views about marriage institution.

'Let people make their free choice between the two options. We shouldn't fight over it,' she said.

'Oh, certainly. We shouldn't make it personal. Tell me, how you managed your break up. Weren't you emotionally traumatized?' I asked her.

'I was really very upset for some time, but gradually learnt to control my emotions,' she said. 'I feel, one shouldn't allow her emotions to hamper progress in life. People should know break up with one person isn't the end of life. You may get some other guy to love you. And the same thing is true for a boy.'

'How long are you going to stay here? She asked me to change the topic.

'I've come to attend my nephew's marriage,' I informed her.

'Trine-Trine,' the sound of the doorbell broke my musings to regain my consciousness. I got up to open the door. I was pleased to see Raj, standing before me. His white hair with wrinkled face was pronouncing withering of his youth charm.

'Hi dear, how're you?' Asked Raj.

'Very fine. I'm happier seeing you hale and hearty and standing in one piece before me,' I said.

'You still look the same as I saw you last time- slim and fit,' Raj commented cheerfully, while hugging me affectionately.

'My dear friend, it takes a lot of efforts and pain to maintain physical fitness. Your romance with food and all goodies in life are bound to take a toll on your shape and size,' I said.

'Dear, you can't change yourself,' Raj said smilingly.

'You didn't change yourself a bit, how can I. You know, I'm not less fussy than you…'

'I'm feeling hungry and I think breakfast time is over,' Raj said interrupting me. 'It's already 11 a.m. and I haven't eaten anything so far.'

In my musing, I'd lost the sense of time.

'You're right. Breakfast time is over. So what! We may order from room service. What would you like to have?' I enquired from Raj.

'I think, milk, cornflakes, toast and tea may be sufficient for me. What about you?' Raj responded.

'I may also take the same. Let me place the order,' I said and lifted the intercom receiver to contact room service.

'Don't place any order,' suddenly Raj said. 'Let's go out and take breakfast at our old restaurant near the Library point. It isn't very far away. We can just walk down.'

I agreed and we both left for our old favourite restaurant.

It was slightly cloudy and cool breeze was blowing. No pullover was required, a half sleeve sweater was enough.

Raj broke the silence, asking, 'Who're the guys to report so far?'

'Many people have reported. However, among our old gang, we're the first to reach here so far. I think, others may join us by lunch time,' I informed him.

'Have you any idea about the program schedule?' He asked.

'Yes, I've seen the program schedule. It simply says, all are requested to be present in the conference room, located in basement, by 10.30 a.m. One of the attractions is the release of the book, written by our generalist friend Mr Sudhir. This is on our college history to commemorate the silver jubilee of our graduation.' I informed him.

'So, we may be free by the lunch time.'

'Yes, and we may go back to our pavilion after that.'

'Raj! Do you remember Mr Kumar, who was teaching us admin in the Academy? Is there any news about him?' I asked, changing the subject.

'Mr. Kumar is fine and may retire in next two years. He's in search of a girl for marriage of his son, who is now more than thirty three years old. He doesn't want his son to repeat his mistake of having love-marriage,' Raj said.

'You know, the biggest irony of life is that everyone thinks he's the wisest person in this world. He won't commit the mistake others have done. But, history keeps on repeating itself...'

'May be what you say is true,' Raj said interrupting me. And after a pause, he again started speaking, 'Mr. Kumar doesn't want his son to have live-in relation. But, he forgets that the present generation is escapist. They're very selfish than what we used to be. They want to have all fun of life without having any liability, so they prefer live-in relation rather than getting married. Perhaps, their philosophy is if you can get fresh milk every day why to taste the stale one.'

'You shouldn't demean the young generation. Have some respect for them,' I said, disagreeing with him. 'Remember your old days. Your parents used to say the same thing about you what today you're saying about the new generation.'

'Believe me. They're really very selfish,' he asserted. 'They always look for comforts and fun. They may love only those people who can provide them all comforts of life. They resist accepting any family responsibilities. The live-in relation is their new haven for meeting their physical needs without discharging parental responsibilities.'

'There's hardly any difference between old and young generation, except that they're less Hippocrates and live in a society which's much liberal compared to that of our time. Remarriage isn't a taboo and live in relations are getting higher social acceptability. Females are less shy and open in demanding marital pleasure. It doesn't mean that females weren't having any desire in the past and they've discovered their happiness overnight. They kept their emotions suppressed due to irrational social and religious taboos and beliefs...'

'We've reached to the restaurant, so hold on your ammunition to fire at me later on,' said Raj, while interrupting me.

'I see this restaurant has defied the law of change. It's the same, as it used to be in our old happy Academy days,' I observed, while glancing around the dining hall of the restaurant.

'It appears so,' said Raj, while looking around the restaurant.

'Let's sit at that corner table, our favourite place from where we can have full outside view,' I suggested and moved towards that direction.

Raj followed me in agreement and we both occupied the corner table.

'Good morning Sir. What would you like to have? Very politely asked the waiter, whose name plate was exhibiting his name as 'Ram Singh.

'Ram Sing, what can you serve us as veg- breakfast? Asked Raj.

'Stuffed-Parathas, Aloo-Puri, Idli, Dosa or Bread-Toast, as you wish,' the waiter rattled through the menu.

'Oh, very surprising! You've started serving south Indian dishes also. I'll like to have Dosa. What about you? Raj asked me.

'Sir, we've been serving south Indian dishes for many years,' Ram Sing informed us respectfully.

'Raj I think, we're wrong in saying there isn't any change in this restaurant, since we left Mussoorie. The menu is a big change. Now, there's hardly any place, where you don't get idli *or* Dosa. South Indian dishes are now equally loved by the north Indians. In my home, once a week south Indian dish is a must. My wife is so fond of idli that she can eat it in all the three meals. But, I may prefer to have one Tandori Stuffed-Gobhi Paratha,' I expressed my choice, while commenting about the restaurant.

'Sir! Coffee or tea?' Again asked the waiter.

'Tea for me and coffee for you, is it okay, Raj?' I asked.

'It's fine with me,' said Raj.

'Okay, Sir,' said the waiter and left.

'Raj! Do you remember the incident, when we're having dinner here and Neetu, along with some other lady officers, was sitting in our front table and...?'

'They're discussing your alleged affair with your so called dream girl,' interrupting me, Raj said. 'How embarrassed and apologetic, they felt finding us on their back. How can I forget that scene?'

'Do you know, what happened next day? I haven't told you so far. Ms Neetu met me the next day and apologized for that incident...'

'I'm sure, you aren't lying to me?' Interrupting me, Raj expressed his doubt.

'Come on Raj! Why should I lie to you? Ms. Neetu informed me, 'Jai! You know, Rina is interested in you, but hesitant to speak. She isn't sure about your relationship with Paru.'

'What're you talking about? Paru is just my colleague, as is Rina. I've no intention to date either of them', I said. 'We're just good colleagues. I don't know, why people can't think beyond any relationship. If you keep any female in good humour that doesn't mean you want to have some relationship with her.'

'I'm extremely sorry for the misunderstanding,' Neetu said.

'How come you've never shared this with me?' Raj questioned, while expressing his surprise.

Our conversation was suddenly halted by the waiter's curt voice- 'Your order Sir!' And he started serving us.

The aroma of Sambhar was really mouth-watering, which forced me to say, 'Wish, I should've also ordered some south Indian dish.'

'You can still do so. Should I order idli or dosa for you?' Raj enquired.

'Thanks. I'm sure, I'll enjoy Stuffed Ghobhi-Parahta,' I said.

Bringing the issue back, Raj asked, 'Tell me the truth.'

'What truth?' I enquired, pretending my ignorance.

'Why'd you hide your conversation with Ms. Neetu?' Raj emphatically asked.

'You know, that evening my neighbour Mr. karnik came to my room. He wanted to caution me for having any relation with Rina. He said, 'I've come to know that you're flirting with Rina. You should know, I'm in a relationship with Rina for last one year. She's like your 'Bhabhi.' So don't meddle in our affairs.'

'How'd you come to the conclusion that I'm needling in your relationship?' I quipped.

'People are telling me that these days you're spending lots of time with her,' he said, raising his voice.

'Very strange! You claim that you're having a relationship with her from the last one year, but you don't trust her. You should've asked her first before talking to me. I'm sure you don't respect, your friend, otherwise you shouldn't have behaved like this,' I replied him angrily, with matching pitch of voice.

'I've no intention to indulge in any discussion with you. I just wanted to caution you,' he said and left my room.

'I thought it was crap, so never shared it with anyone, fearing it might get escalated unwittingly. You're the only person with whom I've talked about this incident for the first time. I mentioned this, incidentally. Now, it may be of no significance except to refresh the old emotions...'

'Sir, here is your tea and coffee.' Interrupting our conversation, said the waiter, who came to serve us again.

'Do you need to order anything else?' He politely enquired and waited for our response.

'Thanks, we're done. Please give us the cheque,' said Raj.

Once the waiter left, Raj said, 'You're a bloody fool. You think nobody knew about your spat with Karnik. Next day, it was a news getting around the Academy and we all knew about it. Karnik himself broadcasted it amongst all his friends and one of them informed me about this untoward happening. I didn't enquire about it from you, thinking you yourself might tell me everything. When you didn't mention about it, I also ignored it.'

'Oh, really! People have so much time to revel in such petty things,' I expressed my surprise.

'May it be a trivial and petty happening for you? People, like Shome, can't live without gossiping about such incidents. It was he, who spread this news with his spicy version. Anyhow, forget it,' said Raj.

'Rs.280/- Sir,' said the waiter, while handing over a bill to Raj.

Raj paid Rs. 300/- to the waiter and told him to keep the balance, while leaving his seat. We left the restaurant to go back to our hotel. While walking down, we noticed lots of indiscreet construction had taken place on both sides of the road. It was very inconvenient for the pedestrians to walk along the road, because of continuous stream of vehicles, honking to get their way.

'Raj! Should we take a taxi?' I asked. 'It appears very unsafe to take a stroll on such a busy road.'

'Don't worry. Let's walk. I'm sure, you won't get hurt while walking,' Raj said.

Suddenly my phone started ringing. I checked my mobile and noticed its screen was showing a call from Rocky Saxena. I picked the call. 'Hello! Hi Rocky. Where're you?' I enquired.

'I've reached the hotel and found that your room is locked. Where're you?' Rocky enquired, while informing me about his arrival.

Raj and I came to the Library point for taking breakfast and now we're on our way back to the hotel. We may take another five minutes to reach. You may wait for us either in your room or at the hotel reception,' I said.

'Okay,' said Rocky and ended his call.

'Who has come? Raj enquired.

'It's Rocky,' I said.

'Oh, he's arrived. Good. What's he doing these days? I'm not in touch with him for many years,' Raj enquired.

'He's joined some private company after taking voluntary retirement from the government service,' I informed him.

'What're his children doing?' Raj asked me.

'He has two kids- a son and a daughter. His son is working for some pharmaceutical company after completing his chemical engineering and daughter is doing her management from IIM-Ahmadabad,' I apprised him.

'So, he's almost free from all his liabilities,' Raj commented.

'He's free from the responsibility of educating his children, but his children are still to be married. Marriage and education are the two biggest responsibilities of the Indian parents. Don't you agree?' I said.

'You're right. My children are also to be married,' said Raj.

'What's holding them from getting married?' I enquired.

'They want to get settled first and have enough money to buy all comforts of life before getting married,' Raj said.

'You're right. Marriage isn't their first priority. These days, children want to get employed first and then struggle to rise in their careers. Before thinking of marriage, they want to have enough money power to afford a good house, car, dining out, parties, holidays abroad and many other comforts of modern life, whatsoever money can buy. Secondly, they look for a perfect partner as per their own understanding of perfectness,' I said to make an observation about priorities of the new generation.

'I agree what you say. This's the case with most of the children I knew, including my own son,' Raj said, while agreeing with me. 'These days most of the women also prefer to marry a person having deep pockets. Any one, earning less than her, is not acceptable for an employed woman. My niece says, 'she'll marry with a boy who can buy a diamond ring for her engagement with his one month salary.' So, the boys have no option except to struggle to get suitable employment and work for longer hours to earn enough money to please their sweethearts,' Raj said.

'You know in our times, most of us were looking for just an educated and good looking female, who can take care of the family. Some preferred for a working girl to buttress their financial resources for supporting their families in case of any exigency,' I shared my views.

'Those days, it was the boy who used to call a shot in deciding the fate of a girl in marriage proposals. Girls and their family were scared of their rejection. But things have changed, today it's the girl who decides the marital fate of a boy. Now they're scared of their rejection. Today a girl may prefer her career over her marriage and keep the boy hanging,' Raj said to share his understanding about the priorities of the new generation. 'I knew a few such incidents where girl refused to marry, even after the engagement, jut to better her career prospects. I tell you a story of a city like-Bhopal. A lady refused to marry, even after distribution of her marriage invitation cards, just because she got a job in Japan. She said, 'I prefer my career rather than marriage, where I'm going to lose my freedom. I want to live and enjoy my life on my own terms. I can marry later on, but I mayn't get this opportunity if I don't take it right now.' Raj narrated his first-hand experience of rising assertiveness among modern women ready to compete with men folks in every walk of life.

'I know a boy, who broke his engagement due to interference by his prospective mother-in-law in his day to day life. He said, 'How can I lead my independent life, when her mother has started deciding everything from food to dresses and bed sheet to curtain even before marriage? Things can be worse off after marriage. So, it's better for me to remain single.' I narrated this incident to highlight the importance of the privacy and independence in the life of the new generation. They aren't ready to toe the line of their parents in regard to their personal affairs like marriage.

'I think, girls and boys are asserting their individuality too much. They prefer to have fun in life rather than accepting drudgery of a married life. They like to wait for a perfect partner instead of having compromised marriage,' Raj said.

'People don't realise that nobody is perfect in this world, but they can make a perfect couple by complementing each other. These days young generation can afford to delay marriage. Society has started accepting live-in relations and even the legal system is also recognising it. The females having live-in-relations are getting protection under law. A child born out of such relation is also recognised by the court as a legitimate inheritor of all properties. Secondly, single living is no more an eyesore and divorce isn't a taboo.' I shared my understanding about social-legal development taking place in Indian society.

'I think marriage institution is at risk,' Raj commented. 'I fear, opting of live-in relations by greater number of people may obviate the need of marriage, which used to be an economic protection to female. Now, women are also earning their livelihood, in some cases, they may be earning even more than their husbands. So men are no more sole provider of the family. In such cases, marriage is a much more emotional adjustment rather than economic adjustment.'

'You're right,' I said, while agreeing with him. 'Now live-in relation are socially acceptable. Such relation not only offers an opportunity to meet your natural mating need, but can also provide you almost a legitimate child to inherit your legacy as per the trend in judicial pronouncements. So marriage institution is really in danger.'

'What you say appears very logical and convincing,' said Raj, while appreciating my views.

'It's not only the openness and prurient desire of individuals which is goading live-in relations in the modern society, but also an economic need,' I commented. 'You must be aware about a latest news report, which says that sometime live-in relations are economic compulsion rather than emotional expression. The said news report says, 'In major cities, getting accommodation near the office is a big challenge. So, sharing accommodation with male or female colleagues makes economic sense. That's why some live-in-relations are the result of economic and functional necessity.'

We stopped our conversation, as we had reached to the hotel. We saw Rocky, relaxing in one of the sofas lying in the hotel lounge.

'Hi, Rocky! How're you doing?' Raj and I greeted Rocky.

'I'm fine. What about you?' Rocky enquired, while responding to our greetings.

'I'm good. Hope you enjoyed your journey,' I said while responding to him.

'Journey was comfortable. I reached here just an hour back,' Rocky said. 'Hi, Raj! Seeing you after a long time. Hope you're doing well.'

'Yeah! I'm fine. It's very pleasant to meet you after such a long time. Dear Rocky! Your remembrance had been always reminding me about our old funny days we spent together,' Raj said, while hugging Rocky.

'Stop pulling my leg. No one can change you fatty couch-potato,' Rocky said, while pinching him.

'Dear friends! I got an SMS,' I said, while reading a message from my mobile phone. 'Very shortly our dear friend Mr. Robert is going to join us. Let's go to my room.'

'Where's Robert these days?' Rocky enquired. 'Has he completed his deputation with the World bank?'

'He's very much back from the USA after completing his five year assignment and is now settled in Bangalore,' I informed. 'He's left his old job and working with some MNC for the last three months.'

'He's a very lucky guy to get a good job,' Rocky commented.

We all started climbing up the stairs to my room, which was on the first floor of the hotel. On reaching my room, I opened the door and said, 'You all're welcome here to refresh your old memories with your dear friends.'

'Thanks for your kindness,' Rocky said. 'Jai! Your suite is very good. We can be comfortable here to spend some time together.'

'Please make yourself comfortable. Should I order tea or coffee for you?' I enquired.

'Coffee will be fine for me,' Raj expressed his choice.

'It's okay with me. Rocky! I hope, you may also love to have coffee?' I asked Rocky, who nodded in agreement.

I lifted the intercom receiver and dialled for room service. 'Good morning Sir! I'm Raman from Room service. What can I do for you?' The attendant responded politely from the other side.

'Please send four cups of coffee to my room,' I said to place an order.

'Anything else do you want, Sir? Raman enquired further.

'Please send some cookies along with the coffee,' I said.

'We're three and you have ordered four cups of coffee,' Rocky enquired curiously. 'I hope you haven't done any mistake in placing an order.'

'Ms. Deepika or some other friend may join us any time. That's why I've ordered for four cups of coffee,' I said to explain the reason for ordering four cups of coffee.

'Good, you ordered one cup extra,' Rocky said, while complimenting me.

'You know friends, last month Mr. Robert came to my house in Mumbai and had dinner with us. In light conversation, he disclosed how he got married. I'm sure, you'll be surprised to know about his marriage…

'Oh, you've some spicy thing to share with us, please tell us quickly and don't mystify it,' Rocky said, while interrupting me.

'Have patience. I'm going to apprise you what Robert told me,' I said and started narrating the conversation I'd had with Mr. Robert. One day, Robert came to my home, when we're having some discussion about the children of my brother. After hearing our conversation, he said, 'Jai, your niece won't marry a boy without knowing him well. There's nothing strange in it. In present time, hardly anyone in the cities may marry, without dating. The days are over, when parents used to fix marriage of their children without even consulting them. I'm not sure, whether you know, I didn't see my wife before my marriage. My wife-Julia's father was a school headmaster and my father was a small businessman. Mr. Jacob, one of my father's friends, knew Julia's father- Mr. Francis. One day Mr. Jacob visited our house and started praising Julia for her caring and compassionate nature. In the course of discussion, he suggested my father, 'I strongly feel that Julia should be a very suitable girl for Robert. You must approach Mr Francis for Robert's marriage with Julia.'

'How's family of Mr. Francis and what he's doing? My father enquired.

'Mr. Francis is a headmaster of Marry Convent School,' Mr. Jacob informed. 'He and his wife are very gentle and God loving people. I know them for a long time. I'm sure, you'll never regret getting your son married with Julia.'

'I know, you treat Robert as your own child,' my father said. 'I appreciate your concern. If you recommend Julia for Robert, I'll certainly consider her for my son.'

'There's no hurry. You should discuss this with Robert and take his opinion before proceeding further.' Mr. Jacob suggested to my father.

However, my father didn't care to know my views on this subject. He'd some discussion with my mother and then told his friend, 'I may decide about Julia after meeting Mr. Francis and his family. Robert can't go against our decision. You please organise my meeting with Mr. Francis.'

Accordingly Mr. Jacob organised my parent's meeting with Mr Francis, who agreed to get his daughter married to me. I was in Delhi, when I came to know that my marriage was fixed.'

'You mean to say you hadn't seen or talked to Julia before marrying her,' I enquired.

'Yeah,' said Robert. 'You've heard me correctly. My parents met Mr. Francis and his family. They liked Julia and fixed our marriage. Accordingly, I was informed about my engagement date. In a month's time, we got married and Ms. Julia turned out to be my real dream girl. I hardly had any problem with her after marriage, except some small differences which anyone can have.'

'It looks unbelievable in today's world. A well-educated and highly placed person like you can marry a girl without dating and talking to her,' I said to express my surprise.

'Believe me. I'm telling you the truth,' Robert said very forcefully. 'Why should I tell you anything otherwise? I'm not benefiting. We're old friends, so I'm sharing my feelings with you, particularly in today's context.'

'How come you never mentioned about this earlier?' I enquired.

'This's contextual,' said Robert. 'Today you mentioned about the reluctance of children to get married and their quest for a perfect partner. So, I shared my story with you. People don't realise that no one is perfect. You've to build your relationship based on your sacrifices for your partner. In the last twenty years of our married life, I didn't have any chance to remorse for getting married with Julia. She's an excellent person and my best friend, whom I can share anything and bank on her for everything.'

'Robert, I can simply say, you're a very lucky guy. Thanks to God, who blessed you with such a wonderful sweetheart? I know some people, who'd been dating and even had live-in relations for a couple of years before getting married, taking divorce within two to three years of marriage,' I said without hiding my feeling of excitement and surprise.

'It isn't just a pure luck,' said Robert. 'A happy marriage needs continuous nurturing of relationship through sacrifices. For the happiness of your spouse, sometimes, you do what you don't do otherwise. You may disagree with her and even may have heated discussion for larger family interest, but certainly without humiliating or hurting her. At no stage, she should get the impression that she isn't loved, trusted or respected. Today, everyone wants to get a perfect partner without realising his or her own imperfection.'

'Trine-Trine,' rang the doorbell and I stopped my narration to open the door. It's the waiter. I allowed him to enter the room to serve coffee.

'Please serve coffee to everyone,' said Raj to advise the waiter.

When coffee was being served, there was a knock on the door. I again opened the door. It was Ms. Deepika, who came to join us.

'Hi Jai! How're you? Deepika greeted me with her smiling face.

'You're welcome. See, who all're here and will love to meet you?' I said while welcoming her.

'Hi! Nice to see you all here. How're you?' She wished all other friends present in the room.

'We all're fine, Deepika,' said Rocky. 'It's good, you came early. We've been just chatting and waiting for you. Robert and Ms. Sophia may also join us any time.'

'Please sit down and have coffee,' Raj requested Deepika, while offering his coffee.

'Thanks Raj,' said Deepika. 'Please, you enjoy your coffee. Jai is managing one for me.'

'You know Deepika, I can't take a sip till a beautiful lady like you joins me,' said Raj, while winking at her.

The doorbell rang again. Deepika was fast to get up to open the door.

'It may be waiter,' I said.

Deepika opened the door and exclaimed 'Oh Robert, it's you! Nice to meet you.'

Deepika welcomed Robert, who gently hugged her. And after exchanging greetings, he came in the room along with Deepika.

'Good afternoon everybody, hope all of you've had a comfortable journey and enjoying coffee,' said Robert, while greeting everyone.

'We all're good and now we'll enjoy your company,' I said. 'How did you come so early? You're expected to reach here after lunch.'

'I was to meet someone in Dehradun. However, I postponed my meeting for tomorrow, so I came early.' Robert apprised us, while pulling a chair.

'Good, you came early,' said Rocky.

'Trine-Trine,' rang the doorbell.

I opened the door, it was the waiter, who has brought one more set of coffee.

'How come you brought another cup? I asked the waiter. 'I haven't ordered for it.'

'I saw your guest coming, when I was going out,' he said politely.

'Very intelligent,' I admired him.

'Please serve it to him.' Rocky asked the waiter, pointing towards Mr. Robert.

'Thanks! I don't need coffee. I just drank it before coming here. I was feeling very tired when I reached the hotel. So, after entering my room, I immediately ordered for a coffee,' said Robert very politely.

'Should I clean the table?' Asked the waiter.

'Yes, please do so,' I said.

The waiter removed all the glasses lying on the table and left us saying, 'Please give me a call to clean the table, once you finish your coffee.'

I saw my watch, it was showing 1.30 p.m.

'What about lunch? Should we go to the dining hall or would you like me to order for room service?' I enquired.

'I think we should've our lunch here itself, so that we can enjoy our privacy and can chat freely,' Rocky expressed his opinion.

'It's a good suggestion,' said Deepika supporting Rocky. 'Jai! You may place an order for simple food. We aren't in our twenties when we can devour anything.'

'If you all agree, we can opt for Chinese cuisine,' I suggested.

'Oh, yes! You can order for veg-Hakka noodles, fried rice, mixed vegetables and some non-veg-dish, whichever you may prefer,' said Robert, while giving his suggestion.

I contacted room service and placed an order for lunch as per suggestion, while requesting him to get it served as early as possible.

'How's your family Deepika?' Rocky enquired. 'Hope your children are doing well?'

'Yeah, my children are doing well. The son is studying medicine and daughter is working in ONGC,' said Deepika as a proud mother.

'So, you're free from all the responsibilities,' Rocky commented.

'Oooh no, the biggest responsibility of getting them married is still to be discharged,' said Deepika.

'Why do you call it your-the biggest responsibility? Rocky questioned Deepika. 'These days, children themselves decide about their marriage and just inform parents to solemnise it. So, it shouldn't be your liability.'

'I don't think such an important issue should be left to the free will of children,' said Deepika to counter Rocky.

'Today's children are mature enough to take decisions in their own interest...'

'Your daughter is well settled. Why she isn't interested in getting married?' Robert quizzed Deepika, while interrupting Rocky.

'Trine- Trine,' doorbell rang again. I was about to get up to open the door, but Rocky held my hand and said, 'Jai! Please be seated, I will open the door.'

I sat down. We all started gazing at the door to check who the new visitor was? Rocky opened the door and saw Sophia, who was expected to come any time.

Entering the room, Sophia shook hands with Rocky and greeted everyone present in the room with her known style. 'Hi, everyone! Hope, you all're sharing old sweet memories.'

'You're welcome Sophia to join us,' said Raj. 'Right now we're sharing the miseries of Deepika, who's keen to get her daughter married, but her daughter isn't interested in obliging her.'

'Why's she reluctant to marry?' Sophia also enquired, while expressing her surprise.

'This was just being explained by Deepika, when you pressed the doorbell,' I said.

'Please continue your story,' said Sophia.

'Sophia, hope you didn't have much trouble in reaching this place,' I said, while interrupting Sophia. 'What'll you have tea or coffee?'

'It was a pleasant journey. I checked in an hour before and have come to your room after getting fresh. I've already taken coffee,' said Sophia. 'I need nothing right now. You may please continue your chat.'

'Okay, it's fine. Deepika, now you may tell us your story,' I said.

'My children say, they'll marry when they get their true love…'

'Do they understand the meaning of a true love?' I said interrupting her. 'Can they differentiate between their love and liking? You might have noticed people saying love to travel, love to watch movie, love you, love my mother, brother, sister, wife and so on. We also say, I like that girl, friend, student, book, etc. All these emotional expressions aren't the same. There's certainly an emotional difference in each of such expressions. In my view, love to wife is something more romantic as compared to the feeling of love expressed by a person to his friend. Similarly love to mother is different from love to the wife. Love is certainly more than to say I like this lady.'

'Jai! You're right,' said Robert nodding his head. 'It's believed that 'true lover' is the one who lays down his or her life for the loved ones. A true love demands sacrifices and not just expression or exhibition of feelings. A true lover not only sacrifices his life, but may always be desirous of happiness and wellbeing of his loved one.'

'It's a wonderful description of a true love, I fully agree with you,' I said. 'A true lover will never like to harm his loved one. Incidents of throwing acid over girls will never be committed by a true lover, who don't treat girl as a commodity to be possessed against her will.'

'I consider love for the partner isn't just a romantic emotion, but a commitment to do anything and everything for her wellbeing,' Robert said. 'Such love never weighs the utility of the loved one. Love for me is an honest commitment to respect, honour and care for my darling. You may love your spouse, even if she isn't able to meet your needs due to her sickness. You may remain in love with her, despite living at a distance due to your job requirement.'

'My daughter says, 'I'll marry the day I get my 'soul mate', otherwise, I'll hold my love rather than settling for a compromised marriage,' said Deepika.

'How'll she identify her true love?' I enquired.

'Once I asked my daughter- Rupali, 'how would you find your soul mate?'

'It's easy. Many bells would ring when I encounter my darling, whom I may marry,' said Rupali.

'It's absolutely a mistaken belief that many bells would ring or storm of emotions would rush, when you meet your 'soul mate,' I told her.

'Mom, you don't understand,' said Rupali. 'I can't just marry any person, who doesn't stir my emotions. I want to marry a guy who I can spend with my rest of life and I don't get bored.'

'What do you think? Marriage is all about pure entertainment only,' I said. 'My dear, marriage is sharing of pain and pleasure together. Since life is a bundle of good and bad things, marriage can't be pleasure alone. Yes! You can make it happy with your positive attitude and sincere efforts.'

'Mom! I don't want you to argue with. I've no plan to marry a few years, so let's stop this discussion,' said Rupali and left my room.

'And since then, I refrained from talking to her on this issue,' said Deepika with a grieving expression.

Joining the discussion, Raj said, 'Deepika! People like your daughter believe in saying, 'God nominates partner for you in haven and that one will be a perfect person for you…'

'Such idea is irrational,' said Robert, while interrupting Raj. 'There's no one like a perfect person, who's just waiting for you. Had it been true, there would have been no happy second marriage. Muslim religion permits four marriages, that doesn't mean they don't wish for a soul mate.'

'I think, you're right,' said Deepika, while agreeing with Robert. 'My daughter is one of them, who believes that marriage is made in heaven and solemnized in this world. Everyone is destined, as per his or her destiny, to get one's soul mate. She'll marry when she gets her soul mate.'

Joining the discussion, Sophia said, 'May God bless her with a soulmate. Instead of getting married out of impulsive infatuation, considering someone as your soul mate, it's good to know the qualities of a person, his liking and disliking before deciding to marry…'

'I strongly believe that people, marrying someone on impulsive liking for his or her specific quality at that moment, aren't rational and emotionally balanced,' I said Interrupting Sophia. 'Such people may marry on a spurt of infatuation, without seriously considering nature, character, compatibility, life goals, and parental desires, their strong likes and dislikes, etc. And when they face the hard reality of life in meeting day to day challenges, which lays the foundation of the marital discord, their so called music of love fades. They start blaming each other for their miseries, while rushing to court to divorce the one who was their darling so far.'

'You're right,' said Robert. 'Within one or two years of marriage, such couples realise they aren't made for each other. They'd made a wrong choice and they didn't get a true soul mate. Had she been a right person, there would've been no problem with her. They start fighting for petty things, which they could've otherwise overlooked. Such wrong notion is one of the causes of divorce getting initiated within first two-three years of the marriage…'

Deepika was getting excited as if Robert was echoing her thinking. She interrupted Robert and impatiently said, 'You're correct, Raj. Once relations are sore, you think your soul mate must be somewhere else. And you may rush to the court to divorce your so called beloved partner as fast as possible.'

'You've touched the right nerve,' I said. 'And after getting a divorce, one may again start searching for his soul mate lest someone may snatch her. When infatuation leads someone to marry, he tends to separate for petty reasons, once infatuation fades away.'

'Search for a perfect partner is a mirage and futile pursuit,' said Sophia. 'People say marriage is fixed in heaven and solemnised in this world. I say, marriage is a matter of exercising choice. There isn't one right choice for marriage. It can be a good or bad choice depending on the individual. We should use our wisdom to know what we're looking for in our partner…'

Interrupting Sophia, Rocky said, 'Most of the times, people don't know what they're looking for in their partner. They hardly have time or priority to understand their strong liking or disliking which they can't compromise. It's very desirable for a person to know his strong likes and dislikes to make a more rationale choice. Every young person thinks to get his darling, as God has created one for each of us. They forget that awareness about the virtues, they look for in their partner, may be a good beckon to help them to identify their darling in a more pragmatic way.'

'I agree, it's very rational view,' I said. 'However, unfortunately, many of us aren't having a priority for such a vital issue of choosing a life partner. They've a vague idea of good or bad one. Once I asked my neighbour, 'What type of a girl, would you like to marry? His response was sweet and simple- 'A good girl.'

'What do you mean by a good girl?' I sought his clarification.

'A good girl means – a good girl,' he said innocently.

'What constitute a good girl? You mean good looking, well educated, having house-making qualities or a working girl, well mannered, having concern for family, loves dining out…'

'I haven't thought like this,' he said interrupting me.

'You want to say, you didn't ponder to know how your darling should be,' I said to quiz him.

'Uncle! I'll think about it and let you know,' he said and left my room in a huff, as if he wanted to get rid of me.

'It's a fact,' said Sophia, nodding her head. 'None of us are ever counselled about such a vital subject either at home or in schools. Parents are always worried about studies of their children. We've no culture to guide our children as how to choose one's life partner or deal with marital affairs to lead a happy married life. It isn't a social priority. What you should look for in your partner is hardly an issue to be seriously debated in any family.'

'You're raising a very vital issue affecting people across the board,' said Raj. 'I always heard my grand Ma saying, whenever I touched her feet, "May God give you a long life and bless with a beautiful wife." This's all about a spouse, I heard from anyone in my family since my childhood.'

'I strongly feel that children must be counselled to have a rational approach for choosing a life partner rather than depending on 'destiny', which is a pure gamble,' Rocky said. 'Rationality can be objectively tested, whereas there's no objective test of destiny.'

'What're you talking guys? I've never seen my wife before getting married and I think no other choice could've been better than her,' said Robert.

'Robert! We all know how you got your dream partner, but it was a sheer luck. You got your dream partner as a God gift without any effort on your part,' Sophia retorted back. 'It doesn't happen always in real life.'

'You know, sometime your choice gets influenced by your emotions or infatuation,' said Robert countering Sophia. 'When infatuated, you see everything good about the person and don't like to listen anything against her. The pervasive spell of beauty prevents you, despite all your efforts, to take a rational decision about your dream partner based on individual's nature, habits, cultural, economic and educational background, religious and linguistic limitations.'

'Robert! You make sense,' I said. 'However, it's very likely to couple with a good person if you try to know your partner objectively, as Rocky and Sophia are saying. I tell you some children are really very wise and conscious of the factors affecting healthy relationship. One day, I asked Sri-my son about his perception of life partner. You know what did he say?

'Dad, I'll like to marry a person, who is intellectually honest and passionate for me. She should be intelligent enough to talk objectively about different issues. And I should feel like meeting her again and again'.

'What about her qualifications to manage domestic affairs and taking care of your kids?' I asked.

'She has to have concern for children, parents and friends. In addition, she should possess qualities like- compassion, positive thinking, judicious in money matters, a peace loving and not a querulous personality,' said Sri to explain further his perception about life partner.

'Your wife, being an educated lady, may prefer to pursue her professional career like you. She may also expect you to share domestic burden and look after children as well as her parents,' I said to raise some other vital issues.

'I don't see anything wrong with it,' said Sri. 'If both of us are working, we've to share the pain and pleasure together. The days are gone when wife used to spend the whole of her time waiting for her husband to come back. Now both are working and, in some cases, it's possible wife may excel her husband. One has to be ready for such eventuality. This's the reality of today's life.'

In mid of our discussion, my niece Jia came to our house.

'How come Sri is at home today and sitting with his Dad?' Jia said, while smiling mischievously and putting her bag on the table. 'I'm sure, he must be having some agenda with the uncle.'

'Jia! You shouldn't doubt your elder brother,' I said. 'We're discussing about choosing a life partner...,'

'I'm sorry,' interrupting me, she said. 'I didn't know, you people were deliberating such a serious issue. This seems very interesting. I may love to join, if you have no reservation.'

'You're welcome, if you're willing to share your views on the subject,' I said.

'I agree with you, Dad. She shouldn't be allowed to sit with us, if she's cheeky in sharing her emotions with us,' said Sri.

'Jia! You know, we're brooding over traits of a prospective partner, which one may like to see in his spouse,' I explained to her. 'Sri has shared his thoughts with me. Now you tell us, what sort of a person you may like to marry with?'

'I'm not hesitant in sharing my views about my darling,' she said. 'Listen! He should be honest, sincere, and happy to take care of the kids. Ready to share kitchen-pains without expecting me to cook alone, once I come back home from the office after working eight to ten hours a day. He shouldn't be an angry young man, but a soft spoken gentle man, who doesn't hurt people through his hard hitting tongue. He shouldn't be arrogant, but a humble person with positive attitude in life,' Jia explained very confidently about the qualities of her prospective soul mate.

'Are you looking for a chef, who can feed you well and work as a nanny to look after your kids, besides attending other mundane activities?' Sri mocked Jia.

'Don't pull my leg,' Jia retorted back to Sri. 'I've told you what matters to me in choosing my life partner. My dear brother, you take care of yourself. Hardly any girl may marry you due to your attitude. No self-respecting girl will like her partner to boss over her. You can do it with your sister, as she's no choice but to bear with you.'

'Stop! Don't make it personal,' I cautioned her. 'I'm happy to know both of you've very clear thinking about your life partner. May God bless both of you with a darling of your choice? Tell me, how'll you find such a person?'

'Uncle! It isn't an impossible task, no doubt a difficult one in view of so many limitations of caste, religion, language, economic and social barriers,' she said firmly. 'When I meet people, I screen them through my checklist of traits, which I think, my darling should possess. And you'll be happy to know that I've already found my soul mate,' she said, while giving a mischievous smile and making a face to tease Sri.

'Congratulations! You never mentioned about it to me. When did you meet him?' Sri asked her impatiently.

'I met him in a conference that I attended last year,' Jia informed us. 'Since then we're in regular touch with each other. He's highly qualified, well placed, but very humble. I found him a very soft spoken gentleman. He's very caring and honest person. However, so far I haven't decided to marry him.'

'Oh God! Finally, you've blessed her with a person, who can dance at her tone. Dad! She's been interested in finding a person, who can do what she wants. If she asks him to sit down, he'll be damn happy to oblige; and will get up if she so desires. He'll say day, if she tells so by mistake, albeit it may be night for everyone,' said Sri to make fun of her.

'I'm glad you could very objectively test him. So, what's the hitch in deciding about marriage?' I enquired.

'You know uncle, my parents won't like me to marry out of my caste,' said Jia. 'He isn't of our caste. So, I can't propose him till I get this issue sorted out with my parents.'

'Oh, this's the issue!' I expressed my surprise.

'Should I talk to your parents?' I suggested to Jia.

'No. Not at all! I'll myself discuss with them at an appropriate time,' she said. 'They've to understand that majority of the population falls out of consideration zone, the moment you confine yourself to your caste. How many people do you know of your own caste and status, whom you may like to marry with? You won't like to marry a person below your own socio-economic status, even if he belongs to your own community. Thus the whole world shrinks to a very limited number of people you know through your relatives, friends or matrimonial advertisements. And this won't give you a good option to choose a right person.' Jia expressed her agony and frustration with the social practices restricting marriage choices.

'If your parents don't agree, what'll you do?' I questioned her.

'I'll do my best to convince them,' Jia said. 'I can't say anything right now.'

'It's a very wise decision,' I said. 'You must take your parents in confidence. I'm sure, they'll appreciate your feelings and may agree with your choice, if they find your choice is right and boy belongs to a good family. In India, marriage isn't just a union of two individuals, but also of two families. So families' compatibility is also a prerequisite. Family background does influence and shape attitude and thinking of an individual. It may be very difficult for two persons to adjust, if they come from totally different socio-economic and cultural backgrounds.'

'Uncle, I'm happy to know, you appreciate my feelings and support me. I'll certainly confide to my parents and will marry only with their blessings.' said Jia and left us to chat with her aunt.

'Jia was right,' Deepika commented. 'She shouldn't get married against the wishes of her parents. All the parents desire to see all happiness and comfort visit their children. Most of the parents know their children's nature, their likings and disliking. Sometime, parents know more about their children than children know about themselves. Children should respect the feelings of their parent more than social practices. If parents disapprove choice of their children, they shouldn't ignore their wishes. They should think, it must be in their interest. The parent's choice should be respected by the children, until their decision is biased by age old irrational social beliefs and practices.'

'You've a point- Deepika!' Joining the issue Raj said. 'But, sometimes children don't share their views with the parents. They consider the parents as their biggest enemy. They think parents don't understand them and don't like their happiness. So, they get married against the wishes of their parents. It's also a fact that sometimes parents refuge to be logical or listen to the views of their children. It's tagged as a generation gap and ignored.'

'If most of the well-wishers are objecting to a relation, one should think, perhaps, he's lost sense of rationality due to infatuation…'

'You know, when you like someone, you see everything good and aren't ready to hear anything against her,' Raj said, while interrupting Deepika. 'I'm saying so on the basis of my own experiences. I used to feel bad, whenever my parents or friends cautioned me about my dilly-dallying with girls and suggested to change my conduct. I hated their sermons.'

'This's a universal truth, people don't like unsolicited advices,' I said. 'It's also a fact that sometimes our well-wishers don't act rationally, and their conduct is blighted by outdated customs. What can be a rationale for honour killings of young children by their own kith and kin? Western parts of the State of Uttar Pradesh and Haryana have witnessed numerous homicides of young couples committed by their own loved one, opposing same 'Gotra' or out of the caste marriage without any rationality?'

'Jai! It's a customary practice among Hindus living in northern India to proscribe marriage in the same 'Gotra'. They do so, perhaps, to prevent promiscuity and indulgence in incestuous relations. It's considered desirable for the growth of a healthy society in a village set up, inhabited by the limited households,' Raj argued. 'Now villages have grown in size and number, so it's possible that loving couple mayn't be closely linked with each other. Therefore, one shouldn't oppose marriage simply on the basis of 'Gotra', particularly when marriage within the 'Gotra' isn't opposed by all the Hindu communities. We should treat such cases as aberrations and not normal social happenings.'

'Sorry, Raj! I don't share your view that opposition to inter caste marriage or same 'Gotra' marriage is an aberration,' said Deepika. 'No! It's widely accepted practice across the country. Inter-caste or inter-religion marriages are exception in cities and towns among liberal families. No doubt there's an upswing in such marriages and these aren't fashion of the day, but negligible oddities. Even today, highly educated and affluent section of the citizens prefer to marry their children in their own community. Matrimonial ads, in any Sunday News Papers, are the best testimony of a divided society we've, besides telling the extent caste, sub-castes and religion play a role in key social relations.'

'I fully agree with Deepika,' said Rocky. 'The fragmentation of the society gives an impression that no Indian lives in India. Sad part is that national identity of being 'Indian' first than anything else hasn't been an agenda of any national party so far, even after 68 years of independence of the country have passed.'

'You know Deepika, Indian women have no right to choose her husband, though this right was very much available to them in Vedic times. Denial of choice for the Indian women is a function of some crafty people, who wanted to treat women as a commodity. And that's why, Indian women suffer from a double whammy. First, they don't have their individual identity. They're either daughter of her father or wife of her husband. Secondly, they're treated as a commodity. Father of a girl donates (kannyadan) his daughter, like any other commodity, to the groom in a marriage,' Sophia explained her point of view.

'You're very correct Sophia,' I said. 'Unlike the western world, Indian girl is either someone's daughter or wife. She's no independent identity of her own. She's obliged to protect her chastity before marriage and fidelity after marriage. If she succeeds, she may be worshiped as mother goddess and liable to be condemned as a devil, if she fails.'

'This's the reason, perhaps, the parents try to marry their daughters at the very first opportunity to get rid of their social responsibility,' said Raj. 'Since they want their daughter to marry within their own caste and religion, they don't have many options to choose a compatible groom for their daughter.'

'What you say is also a fact,' said Deepika. 'I think the marriage institution protects Indian caste system, hence society denies women a right to choose their partner out of the caste. Hindu marriage isn't predominant choice based. So, whenever any woman tries to exercise her right to choose her partner, she faces backlash of her family and society in most of the cases, particularly in rural India.'

'I find things are changing,' I said. 'There had been many debates over hon**ou**r killings in all national TV channels. It must've impacted thinking of the Indian citizens. Perhaps growing rationality and general criticism have forced the Khap Panchayats to review their decisions. You must've recently read a news story that Khap Panchayats have allowed inter-caste and same 'Gotra' marriage. You can hope that caste and 'Gotra' barriers may melt down gradually. The age old customs and practices can't vanish in thin air in one day. You may trust the new generation. They are quite mature in their thinking and rational in their decision making.'

'I'm a very optimistic person and fully agree with Jai that we must trust our children,' said Rocky. 'I may like to give full freedom to my children to choose their partner.'

'Rocky, what do your children think about marriage?' Asked Deepika.

'Like your daughter, my children also think that they shouldn't get married till they find their soul mate,' said Rocky. 'It's wrong to get settled with someone, who isn't their true love. So, they want to hold out their emotions for the so called 'true love'.

'What does true love mean to them?' Asked Deepika.

'It means finding a person, who completely meets their wish list, and such person they believe is the best one for them. As per their perception, true love can be found through dating only,' Rocky said to explain the meaning of the true love as per the understanding of his children.

'I married my wife without meeting her before marriage. So, I shouldn't have found my true love, as per the understanding of your children,' said Robert, reacting to the idea of dating. 'On the contrary, I got my true love without any dating. My darling has passion for me. She cares me so much, I can't think to live a day without her. I didn't meet my wife before my marriage. So, there was no way to judge her suitability to become my soul mate. However, present generation can't think of getting married without dating or having relationships. I may tell you an incident. One day, I came home early from my office and found my daughter-Sonia and her friend were chatting in the drawing room.

'What's going on? Can I join you, if nothing personal is being talked over?' I enquired and, without waiting for their reply, sat down on one of the empty couches.

'Dad! You know, Julia is getting engaged, but she isn't happy. Her parents have fixed her marriage without consulting her,' said Sonia to inform me. 'This isn't good. How can her Dad fix her marriage without talking to her?'

'How can I marry a person without knowing him and who isn't my true love?' Julia said in a slightly harsh tone.

'Juila! If you don't mind, may I ask you something personal?' I said.

'Why not? Uncle, you can ask me anything,' said Julia very politely.

'Please elaborate, what do you mean by true love?' I asked her.

'True love for me is a person, who loves and cares for me. He arouses some romantic feelings in me and respects women in general. I should crave to spend my rest of the life with him,' said Julia hesitantly to explain about her perception of a true love.

'How will you find such a person?' I further enquired.

'If someone does have hobbies, habits, nature, likings/ disliking, social status similar to that of mine, he can be my darling. I can meet him in any party, social gatherings or find him through chat on a social media, which offers lots of opportunities to know people across the world,' said Julia.

'People can manipulate their personality and character,' I said. 'There'd been many stories in newspapers about unscrupulous people befriending girls through net chats and diching them. They lured women with marriage promises and later on spoiled their life.'

'Uncle! There're also cases where girls could find their life partners through the internet and are living a very happy married life,' Julia said.

'What you say is also true,' I said. 'I just wanted to caution that chat alone mayn't help you to know the true nature of a person. Words and conduct should've harmony, which can be judged only through personal meetings. And, this may be a risky job. Secondly, similarity in liking and disliking doesn't mean you can love him or he'll be your true love. Marriage gives you an opportunity to know your partner and develop love for him. It gives a unique feeling of being together. So, if one gets married with a good person, love can grow between them and they can turn into a happy couple, even without knowing each other before marriage.' I further explained to her.

'Uncle! You mean to say that it isn't possible to find a perfect person, who matches my definition of true love?' Julia enquired.

'Julia! You should know, there's no perfect person in this world, including you and me,' I said. 'Your definition of true love gives me an impression that true love means a person who matches your definition of a perfect man. And, anything short of finding a perfect person of your imagination may imply failing to get your true love. This appears fallacious, such mind set may lead you to construe a marriage with any person, not matching your criteria of a perfect person, as the sad thing to happen…'

'I don't think, you can be happy marrying a person whom you don't love,' Julia said, while interrupting me.

'You think, you may've horrible married life, if you marry a person without dating and loving him. And, it may be a compromised marriage,' I said. 'It's not always true. When I married, I wasn't aware about the very existence of your aunt, what to say about knowing and matching her traits with that of mine. In my view, it's the honest endeavour of both the husband and wife, complementing each other, make them a happy couple. When you share the pain and pleasure together, you develop true love for each other in due course of time,' I said to explain her the reality of life.

'Uncle! You mean, people can marry without knowing each other and can make a happy couple, forgetting their past,' Julia enquired.

'Yes. In India, many marriages still take place where parents fix the marriage of their children. They don't get any opportunity to meet each other before marriage. There's no guarantee that your dating or live-in relations will turn your marriage into a wonderful achievement of your life. Had it been true, there would've been no dissolution of marriage, when people get married after having live-in relation. Similarly, there is no guarantee that you'll have a very happy life, if you opt for an arranged marriage,' I said to explain her further.

'It sounds very strange but logical. Knowing your case, I tend to believe what you say,' said Julia.

'Actually marriage is dissolution of old relations, bonding and loyalties to give birth to a new relationship, loyalties and bondage. Marriage creates new relationships between two families and two individuals, who may have different desires, hopes, expectations, values and goals in life...'

Interrupting me my daughter-Sonia asked, 'Dad, do you think, it's possible to forget your past relations so easily and lead a happy married life without facing any family dispute in future?'

'I think, sometimes, old relationship leads to a big conflict and spoils your marriage,' I said. 'It mayn't be easy for your partner to forgive you for your past conduct. So, it's better to share your past with your partner before committing to marriage. And forget your past, if he accepts you. Albeit, it mayn't be easy to do so.'

'Most people are scared of sharing their past. They fear, they may lose a friend or spoil their marriage,' said Sonia to express her apprehension.

'What you say is true. Your generation has to accept that there can be hardly any person without friends and all friendships can't turn into marriage. So past relations shouldn't be allowed to become an eyesore, having a potential to wreck your family. No doubt, such issues are bound to cause differences and conflict in relationships, but they need to be managed and not buried. The unresolved differences, if suppressed for long, may erupt like volcanoes and rock the bottom of your marital relation,' I said to explain my views.

'You're right, Dad, every individual has friends and all friendships can't metamorphose into marriage. So, past relations may trouble anyone and destroy marital happiness. So what should be done?' Asked Sonia.

'Emergence of conflict shouldn't be feared, but should be taken sportingly to sort them out at the very first opportunity to develop deep understanding between the couple. This'll help you to develop love and respect for each other, besides cementing your marital relations. Timely management of conflicts may brace you up to face adverse swings in your life in a more effective manner. Couples, who don't work out their differences to manage their conflicting issues, are vulnerable to divorce,' I further explained.

Julia suddenly jumped and hugged me saying, 'Thanks a lot uncle! You've opened my eyes. Now, I've different understanding of marriage. I may consider marrying the person chosen by my parents.'

'I wanted to share this incident with all of you to point out that everyone has his or her own understanding of the marriage and true love,' said Robert. 'It has become a fashion to spend time with different persons in search of a so called true love, without understanding the meaning of a true love. It isn't a quest for a true love, but a longing for all the materialistic and the titillating fun in illusion of finding a true love.'

'In fact, what Julia was thinking of a true love is a reflection of consumerism, where consumer preference to any product is defined through his liking for the product,' I said, while agreeing with Robert. 'You may prefer someone whose attributes or some qualities you may like, because of their potential to please you, in the same way as you may respond to a product you like. This consumerist approach is becoming an essence of the modern relationship amongst the young generation. You may like someone at a moment, but another moment you may discard her as you discard the product once its utility diminishes or fades.'

'In my opinion, one shouldn't enter into marital relation expecting more than a normal human being can deliver. If you expect your darling to exhibit, dozens of attributes, though there may be some exceptions, chances of getting you frustrated are destined to be high,' said Sophia.

'I fully support you, Sophia,' said Robert. 'Similarly, if you expect your wife to treat you like 'Pati-Parmeswar'(GOD), you need to love her like 'Devi'(Goddess). You may fail in doing so, but you mayn't tolerate her failings in respecting you.'

'I agree with both of you. Paradoxically, we expect our darlings to respect and worship us, ignoring the corresponding obligation of giving love and respect to them by discharging the responsibility of a 'Pati-Parmeswar,' I said supporting their point of view.

'Trine-Trine,' doorbell rang. I got up to open the door.

'I think waiter has brought the food,' Raj said.

I opened the door. It was the same waiter with a food trolley.

'Please come in,' I said. The waiter entered into the room with food trolley.

'Sir, should I serve the food? Asked the waiter.

'The talks have been so interesting, intensive, and involving that we forgot the time. I think, we should eat our lunch. I'm feeling very hungry,' said Rocky.

'Oh, yes,' said Deepika. 'Please serve the food, otherwise Rocky may break our head. He is getting hangry.'

The waiter started serving the food. And after serving the food, he said, 'May I take your leave, if you don't need anything else?'

'You can, but please come after half an hour to clean the table,' I said.

'Yes Sir.' He confirmed and left the room gently.

All appeared to be very hungry, so started devouring the food as if they hadn't eaten anything since for long.

Breaking a long spell of silence, Sophia admired quality of food. 'The food is very tasty. How do you like it, Deepika?'

'No doubt, food is very good,' said Deepika. 'It isn't very spicy and oily. It tastes like home cooked food.'

'One feels comfortable in known territories. It's true about food also. Generally, one mayn't like to adventure for new cuisines,' said Rocky.

'It's human to be happy and comfortable with known things. Most of us have a fear of the unknown, and that's why, hesitant in initiating a dialogue with a stranger,' said Robert.

'Let us enjoy the food. Jai, I came here to get some juicy and spicy news about our old folks, but I'm really surprised to get such a heavy discourse,' said Sophia.

'We enjoy food every day, but we miss this company. We hardly got a chance to see you after your departure from India. We're meeting you after college. And today's discussion has really helped us to open up. Sophia, don't you think so?' Rocky commented, while expressing his happiness to meet Sophia after such a long span of time.

'Yes, you're right, Rocky,' said Sophia. 'Thanks for this meet, otherwise, we couldn't have got a chance to peep in each other's life and know something very personal. No doubt, I'm meeting all of you after college, except Jai. I met him incidentally in one of the wedding party, I attended a few years back.'

'Should I order something more or it's enough?' I enquired.

'I'm full. The food is really very tasty. I've over eaten,' said Robert, while putting his plate on the table.

'I think, I need a second filling,' said Rocky and got up to dish up some more vegetables and bread on his plate.

In fifteen minutes, everybody finished the food. 'Will you prefer to take tea or coffee or dessert? I enquired.

'I may prefer coffee than eating any dessert, besides it can keep us engaged too,' said Deepika.

Everyone consented to have coffee. So, I lifted the intercom receiver and ordered for coffee, while requesting phone attendant to send the room boy to clean the table.

'Today's lunch discourse has been so engrossing, I may remember it for the rest of my life, and may share it with my other friends and families,' said Sophia.

'I think, I've over eaten and mayn't enjoy coffee,' said Robert, requesting me to cancel coffee for him. Hearing this, Rocky and Sophia also refused to drink coffee. Following them, Deepika asked me to cancel the entire order. 'Jai, you may cancel the entire order. We can wait for some time to go for coffee.'

I cancelled the order for coffee and requested the attendant to send the room boy to clear the table.

Restarting the discussion, Raj tried to find an answer to his dilemma. 'If we extend the analogy of 'fear of the unknown' to marital relations, one shouldn't part with his existing partner to find a new one. We see rising divorce cases and, at the same time, people are getting married. How would you explain this dichotomy-Rocky?'

'Marriage is like a sweet. Whosoever tastes it bemoans and who doesn't also repents. What do you think-Jai? Will you agree with me?' Rocky said jokingly, while looking at me.

'Infatuation' and 'sensuous lust' are naturally ingrained in human beings. It may be a cause of this dichotomy,' I said.

'You meet someone and like some of her attributes at that moment and think you got your darling. Once emotionally infected, you aren't able to see or rather tend to ignore your red flags. You get married, when infatuation fades away so called fabulous relation starts disappearing…'

Interrupting me, Sophia said, 'You are very right. Once infatuation is over, the very romantic union soon becomes an agonising prison, which one wants to escape at the first given opportunity. Every young man, waiting for the marriage, thinks he won't commit the same mistakes others have done, but history repeats. Who can say this better than me? Once, my relation with Subbu deteriorated, I wanted to get rid of him as early as possible.'

'I've a slightly different view,' said Rocky. 'Since human beings are very selfish, I strongly feel, marriage is also a selfish foray undertaken by the two individuals for satisfying their desires of raising a family and meeting sensual needs.' Rocky put forward his point of view about marriage.

'If you treat marriage as a selfish act, in that case everyone of us commits mistake of marrying a selfish person like you.' I said.

'If what Rocky says is considered true, it may be difficult for two selfish people to make a happy couple. It is possible one may've some annoying habits and nature similar to that of you. And all such annoying traits you may discover only *after* marriage, which offers opportunities for such revelations in intimate moments and context. So, we all're bound to have some sort of a compromised marriage with a person, who mayn't always be capable to meet our individualized and selfish whims. When one doesn't meet our expectations, we think he isn't the 'darling' we dreamed of every day,' said Sophia, responding to Rocky.

'It means one shouldn't marry as two selfish souls are bound to make life a hell,' I said.

'What you say have some substance. However, you mayn't disagree that marriage is also a social obligation. If you don't marry, society may consider you physically challenged to produce a progeny. So many parents force their children to marry. Villagers force their miner daughters to get married, as early as possible, the moment they attain puberty,' said Deepika to raise a social dimension of the marriage.

'It's also a fact that neighbours, friends and relatives make life miserable, if your children aren't getting married after attaining their adulthood. So, as a parent, you start persuading your children to get married, what may happen after marriage mayn't be your concern at that moment,' said Robert to highlight peer pressure on parents for getting their children married as early as possible.

'It's very strange to know parents getting their daughters married without ascertaining credential or the interest of the grooms. In such cases, women either get divorced sometime after the marriage or suffer all through their life just to save their parents' social prestige and dignity,' said Rocky

'No doubt what you say is also a fact of life, but there's a remarkable change in the marriage pattern,' said Sophia. 'In cities, children aren't in a hurry to marry. Girls are delaying their marriage. They want to settle before getting married. Since they are getting employed, they expect their partners to earn more than they do. So, boys are delaying their marriage as it takes time to get settled.'

'You've a point, Sophia. Girls are also delaying their marriage due to their career pressure. Actually marriage is both a pain and a pleasure. It's an incredibly fun and also incredibly pain too. Particularly, when there's a discernible change in gender role,' said Robert, while trying to explain gender role in marriage. 'Traditionally husbands used to be the provider of a family, in the changed economic scenario, now wife may also be a bread earner of a family or sole provider. But traditional husbands still want their wives to submit, respect and treat them as 'Patiparmeswar'. This creates fissures and marital discords, if not handled wittingly in time.'

'So, we find ourselves in the midst of a massive shift in marriage trend, women waiting longer than ever to marry a perfect person. They hold out their love for their true soul mate. Sometime, she may miss a nice person who may ask for a date and she turns him down, if the sparks of attraction aren't hot from the start. One doesn't realise that with every passing day, particularly after the passage of thirty springs of life, chances of getting married diminish. And a time comes, when she is ready to marry with someone less deserving, but don't find any willing soul to accept her as a spouse,' said Deepika.

'You have a point,' said Robert. 'If you're holding out your relations for perfection, or have a long list of must-have traits for your spouse to possess, it's possible, you're overlooking some good persons, who are already in your life. In this context, you may recall a famous Hindi movie 'Parineeta', where hero wasn't aware about his love for his childhood friend. He realised it when someone else came into her life and he feared to lose her forever. Finding out a potential mate is worth appreciating, but wasting time just for a perfect partner isn't appreciable.'

'No doubt, every marriage inevitably calls for some compromise on one part. I consider marriage decision a sort of throwing a dice in the gamble,' said Rocky. 'And you don't know what would be the result. Nevertheless, like any decision, marriage decision needs to be taken rationally. So, I consider indecisiveness for marriage as a sign of inability on the part of an individual to shoulder parental responsibilities. While taking a decision about marriage, one may consider values like intellectual honesty, sacrificial-love, man's capacity to provide, good reputation, character, loving and caring nature and family back-ground etc. However, one must know his or her strong likes and dislikes, so that a mature decision is taken based on prospective dream partner's nature and habits.'

'Sometimes decision making is influenced by personal preferences for a role model as a husband or wife,' said Sophia. 'One may like to marry with a person who's like a famous cricketer, tennis player or a movie actor. If you want your husband to possess traits of numerous personalities, it may be very challenging to take a decision based on rationality...'

'You're very right,' said Deepika, while interrupting Sophia. 'In this context, I get reminded about an incident, which I may like to share with all of you. One day, I was chatting with my daughter. Suddenly she said, 'Mom! Gauri must be very lucky. She got a very charming and romantic husband like Shahrukh Khan.'

'My darling! Gauri never married Shahrukh Khan, as you know him today,' I said. 'She married a person, who was just like your next door neighbour struggling for survival. Today he's a famous actor. You should remember that wives of famous persons didn't marry individuals, whom world know today as their husbands. They married simple guys, who became role model for others over a period of time. This must have obligated the wives to sacrifice their so many desires to make their husbands what they're known today.'

'I think you're absolutely right Mom. I never thought about it. How come one gets a good husband?' Inquired my daughter.

'It may be a matter of luck. However, one should choose her partner wisely. While deciding about partner, you should see the potential of a person to become something, what you admire or cherish. The potential for growth may be strongly evident, but it's yet to be fully realized,' I said.

'What a wonderful observation you made,' said Rocky. 'It'll be equally true for boys also. A boy shouldn't get impressed with outward appearances of a girl like her good look, status, designer jewellery or dresses, property, social status, etc. Instead, he should explore her inner quality like-innocence, honesty, sincerity, commitment, and caring concern. These're the real treasure and don't vanish with the passage of time.'

'Every young and unmarried person, be male or female, starts wondering, after reaching the age of adolescence, "Is someone made or destined for me? Or do I have to choose one amongst those I encounter through my life-journey," said Robert. 'No doubt, such questions, I also had like any other young person in my college days. But, now I firmly believe that one can live happily with any person, if his choice is made rationally. You can know for certain, whoever you wed becomes your darling, if you commit to her and don't have the illusion of a fairy love.'

'People think joy in marriage is all about a choice you make- who to marry, rather than realising the true joy is in complementing each other to become a perfect couple,' said Sophia.

'You're saying a very sensible thing. We find many examples of people getting married without seeing each other and living a very happy married life like me,' said Robert. 'Theoretically, it's possible to have good married life with more than one person. This's convincingly proved with abundant examples of happy second or third marriage. Had God made only one person for you, there would've been no second marriage after the demise or divorce of the first partner.'

'I think life is based on common sense. Unfortunately, most of the marriage conflicts are the result of absence of the common sense,' said Sophia. 'Sometimes in a fit of rage, one of the partners may say something, which may emotionally disturb the other partner. He may snap the communication causing breakdown of normal relations. It's the communication skill which alone differentiates a human being from the rest of living creation of God. So, you need to use communication skill to be human. And, the communication alone can help you in solving the disputes. Hence common sense says, one shouldn't snap the communication and things said in a heated moment shouldn't be taken by the heart to break the normal relations. I'm saying all this on my own experience.'

'It's a great piece of advice,' said Deepika. 'A similar etiquette was suggested by my mother to both of us at the time of our wedding, when she told us, "You listen when your husband speaks, and he should when you speak. If you follow this, you can lead a very happy married life."

'It's an amazing guidance for a married couple. What I'm saying is my personal experience. Had Subbu, my first love, not taken my simple comments so seriously to break communication, today we could've been together?' said Sophia, with a deep breath. Perhaps, her heart still beats for her first love.

'Do you regret your break up with Subbu?'I asked

'No! It's not an issue, whether I regret or not.' said Sophia. 'The main issue is giving undue importance to trivial things, which doesn't deserve that importance. Your relation is the most important thing than winning or losing an argument or prestige before your family members or friends. Some argument is always better than having no dialogue. Differences give you an opportunity to appreciate the other's point of view and develop a deeper understanding about him. So one shouldn't resort to snapping of dialogue to suppress the differences or conflicts. Discords should be managed and not suppressed by keeping them under the carpet'.

'I fully agree with Sophia. Conflict is inevitable in any relation between two persons, be it husband-wife, father-son, friends or partners in business, because two persons don't share the same values, expectations, desires and ambitions in life. Conflict is a part of relations, and it should be taken as an opportunity to know others and adjust with their habits, values, and ways of functioning,' Raj said while agreeing with Sophia.

'Raj! I'm also in agreement with you,' said Rocky. 'Two people don't have the same expectations, thoughts, opinions or needs in life, so conflict and dispute are natural to occur in any relations. I see merit when Jai says one should never fear conflict, but face it with full honesty and an open mind. It may give you an opportunity to see the life from the other's vantage point for making better adjustment to harmonize your energy for mutual benefits. If you try to correct your partner to make her like you, perhaps, you may end up not having her.'

'I think we all may agree with what Sophia, Raj and Rocky are saying. Life has 360 angles. What we see and face, we believe that's the truth and disagree with others, what they see and believe. Whereas, both are correct and both know partial truth. So, if we don't try to correct others in life, we mayn't have much discords and differences. Try to understand the other's point of view. If we're able to see the good side of life, endeavor to show others that face of life, instead of correcting them without showing other side of the coin. If we follow this simple approach, most of our conflicts may vanish in thin air, not only in the family, but also in another sphere of life,' I said.

'Jai! At this juncture of life, we understand things better than what we're capable at our teens. At that age, we had limited exposer of life,' said Raj, who kept silence for some time. 'Study was our main task and we considered that a big burden. And, the parent's objection to any outing was a big eye sore. Every good looking female was subject of a passionate discussion among friends...'

'If possible you could've married all of them,' I said, while interrupting him.

Everybody present in the room burst into laughter. Raj could hardly smile as he felt uncomfortable.

'Jai. Don't make him butt of fun. We shouldn't make it personal,' said Sophia.

'I'm sorry Raj. I've no intention to hurt you...'

'You look very handsome, when you keep silent. I'm telling myself, what I think, so don't take pain to speak for me,' said Raj, expressing his displeasure.

'Jai, don't disturb him. Let him speak,' said Sophia.

'I've no hesitation in accepting that I'd had many girl-friends before marriage. You all know this,' said Raj, while resuming his conversation. 'My relation with any girl didn't last for more than a year at best. I used to compare my every new girlfriend with my previous one. Most of the time, I would find some shortcomings in her. I didn't appreciate no one is perfect in this world. And every one might've some qualities, but not all I was looking for. I didn't realise that I'd to compliment my dream girl to make our relation perfect and dependable. Jai used to object my every new relationship and break up too. I never realised that nurturing relations with many girls may mess up my married life. I broke my first marriage basically on two counts. First- after marriage, I consistently compared my wife with my ex-girlfriends and used to rue marrying her, thinking I should've married with my first girlfriend. Second- my past relations didn't allow me to enjoy the consummation of marriage. I often thought, my wife must have slept with someone. And this very thought used to kill me every day. Consequently, my behaviour became very awkward and quirky, which puzzled her and became a major cause of her trepidation. Gradually our relationship touched a nadir of distrust and every small issue started getting flared up to widen our discards and distrust. And eventually, one day we mutually decided to divorce. Our marriage survived, barely two years, and hardly a day passed when we didn't have any issue. Our marriage could've been easily saved, had I demonstrated some maturity and used common sense. Having realised life was a mirage or a gamble and it would be futile to chase a perfect partner, I married with Sushma without much fuss. I couldn't prevent all this, just because I lacked common sense, what Sophia just mentioned about.'

'Raj! Don't make it personal. We're just sharing our experiences and what's happening in our society at present,' said Sophia, while consoling Raj, who became quite emotional.

'No! I'm not making it personal. I'm also sharing, what life has taught me. Perhaps the sharing of experiences may save other lives by not repeating my misdeeds,' said Raj. 'You know, I chose Sushma, a girl from small town, as my second wife. She's a very conservative lady, who won't hesitate to touch my feet in the presence of hundreds of people. She'll keep various types of fast and do Pujas for my longevity and happiness, without realising how much I hate her observing rituals. I never dreamed of having such a devoted Indian woman as my darling in my life.'

Everyone was spellbound in listening Raj, who paused for a moment and took a long breath before further narrating his story. 'I think, luck also has a vital role to play in what you get from your life. See! Robert is the happiest person to get his dream girl, even without seeing or meeting her before marriage. And on the other hand, I'm unhappy despite befriending umpteen number of girls before marriage in search of a perfect soul mate. I couldn't get that happiness, even marrying twice after having a thorough examination of each girl, what Robert got without seeing or meeting his darling before marriage.'

'Past relations do matters. I know a boy snapping relations with his wife within a fortnight of his marriage. He told his parents that he didn't believe in marriage institution and wanted to divorce his wife. His parents were shocked and petrified thinking about the consequences. See, the apathy of the boy. More than 30 years old young man couldn't empathise with the fate of his wife, who left her family to join him with a hope to have a happy married life. His weirdness was attributable to the cunning behaviour of his ex-girlfriend, who wanted to have live in relations with him rather than getting married,' said Rocky.

'Such cases are increasing. And ex-relations are also becoming a potential cause of extramarital affairs. An ex-boy or girlfriend provides an easy access to one, who is either frustrated in one's married life or wants to get out of the rut to spice up one's life or looking for emotional support,' Said Sophia.

'New generation has no remorse for prurience. As per the Times of India report, 37 million members of the Ashley Madison, a website offering romance outside the marriage, embraced the website tag line "Life is short. Have an affair". Such a large membership is a testimony that YOLO generation attaches no guilt emotion to sexual desire. These changes in society herald a social behavior that infidelity, which existed since the inception of the marriage institution and condemned widely, is no more immoral or a sin. It's now far more socially acceptable,' I said, quoting the said news report.

'Yes. Technology has helped the people to come closer and have an easy access to the so called liberal clubs,' said Raj. 'Many websites are offering ample opportunities to cheat or enjoy the excitement of a fling while being in marriage. The internet has made cheating a far easier option than ever before.'

'Besides the internet, modern economic compulsion and the market economy have obligated people to work longer hours with opposite sex under one roof. This creates perpetual stress and leads people to spend less quality time at home or family relationship. If people spend more time with colleagues in office than with a spouse, it's natural to get attracted and have an affair outside the marriage,' said Robert to make his observation.

'These developments may give an impression that marriage institution is irrelevant, but it's still considered the best option by both the sexes as a reliable way to get social respectability, family, companionship and economic support despite its shortcoming,' said Deepika.

'Trine-Trine,' doorbell rang. Deepika stopped and asked me to open the door. 'Jai, will you please go and see who has come?'

I got up and opened the door. 'Sir, can I clean the table? Sorry for being late,' said the waiter, who was standing at the door.

'You're welcome. Please remove all the utensils and clean the table,' I advised the waiter.

I saw my watch, it was showing 4 p.m.

'It's tea time. Will you like to have tea or coffee?' I enquired.

'I think, I would like to go to my room and take some rest. Today, we've a very long and unusual discussion. I feel totally exhausted and want a break,' said Sophia.

'I think, I should also rest and meet you at the dinner time,' said Deepika, while getting up to leave my room.

'You're right. We should stop our discussion here and let us meet at dinner around 8 p.m. in the dining hall,' I suggested.

Everybody agreed to the suggestion and left for their respective room, except Raj.

'Raj! What's your plan? Will you go to your room or take some rest here?' I enquired from Raj, who was exhibiting no sign to leave my room.

'If it isn't disturbing you, I may prefer to spend some more time with you,' said Raj.

'You know, we're meeting after a long time. It'll be my pleasure to chat with you for some more time,' I said.

'Please order for coffee and some cookies,' requested Raj.

I lifted the intercom receiver and placed an order for two cups of coffee and some cookies to be served in my room. I noticed Raj wasn't happy.

I enquired, 'Raj! Are you okay? You appear a bit disturbed. I think you should take some rest. You must be tired due to long road journey.'

'No, I'm fine. Actually, I'm deliberating over what we discussed today about various facets of a marriage and soul mate. I am trying to figure out where I've gone wrong in choosing my life partner. Since my childhood, I'd some image of my darling. Whenever I saw any beautiful girl, I used to examine her from that perspective. I met numerous girls in my life and mayn't even remember their names. Hardly, any of them matched with the traits of my dream partner. So, my both the marriages had been a sort of compromised settlement,' said Raj to share his deep rooted emotions with me.

'Why're you saying so? You got a good charming wife, who cares a lot for you. Your children are educated and may get settled soon. You should feel thankful to God,' said I to console him.

'You won't appreciate my feelings, Jai!' He said very emotionally.

'If you don't tell me what really bothers you, how can I know your problem?' I countered him.

'You know, I was in love with Pratibha and actually wanted to marry her, but couldn't do so. You know why?' He said.

I was amazed to observe a twinkle in his eyes, when he mentioned about Pratibha, as if his long cherished desire was fulfilled.

'Tell me. Why didn't' you marry her?' I enquired while suppressing my anxiety and curiosity.

'Please listen carefully and don't be stupid to disturb me in between. I still remember the whole incident, as if it happened yesterday. It was a beautiful summer night at the Academy. We finished our dinner and left the dining hall for our respective hostels. Suddenly, Pratibh said, 'Raj! It's a very clear sky with a very bright moon. The breeze is very soothing and romantic. I would love to take a stroll, if you give me your company.'

'I think, I may equally enjoy your company in this beautiful weather. Let's walk in the garden,' I suggested. And we started walking towards the nearby garden, holding hand-in-hand. We didn't speak for a while and moved in complete silence, as if we became one soul and two bodies.

'Raj! I think, it's a full moon and that's why it's looking so bright and pretty,' she said, while interrupting the silence.

'You may be right, but I'm not very sure. No doubt moon is very bright and charming, but you're looking prettier than moon,' I said and pressed her hand.

We walked holding each other's hand up to the fountain, located at the centre of the garden. It used to be a lonely place, particularly at night. We walked to the side benches, where hardly anyone may venture in night. We sat down on a corner bench. She came closer to me and said, 'Raj! In a month's time, we'll be moving to our respective work places.'

Very gently, I placed my left hand on her left shoulder, while pressing her left hand with my right hand. 'Still a month to go. Why're you so worried? Enjoy this beautiful moonlight. Right now, you shouldn't think of parting but for union,' I said and kissed her. She didn't resist my kissing and hugged me very warmly. We both kept on kissing each other for a few minutes. Suddenly, she pulled herself back and started staring at me. I again pulled her closer to my chest and kissed her. She responded very warmly. I got passionate and pressed my hand on her back. She also clinched my back. She started opening my shirt's button, while kissing me. After opening my shirt, she started kissing on my bare chest, while holding firmly my both the shoulders. This aroused me. I embraced her tightly and loosened her bra. We kept on kissing each other for some time, and suddenly we broke all barriers to unite. When we regain our senses, she asked me, 'Raj! Hope you'll marry me soon.'

'Why not? Very soon we'll be together. I can't think of living without you. I love you,' I said and kissed her.

'Let's go back,' she said.

'Okay,' I nodded and we both got up. We cared our clothes and started walking towards her hostel hand-in-hand. We hardly spoke. When we reached close to her hostel, I left her hand. She kissed me and started moving towards her room. I pulled her back and kissed her.

'Please leave me, someone can see us,' she said, while pulling her shelf away from me.

'Okay,' I said and left her hand.

'Good-night, see you again,' she said and moved to her room.

'See you tomorrow, good night,' I said and started moving towards my hostel. On reaching my room, I opened the door. As I entered my room, I saw a letter from my father, which was perhaps pushed into my room from a cleavage beneath the door. I opened it to get a message that my father wanted me to marry his friend's daughter- Teena. She was studying in London, where her father was working in the Common Wealth Secretariat. I clinched the letter and sat down. I started brooding over what'd happened between me and Pratibha a few moments back. I didn't have courage to say no, either to my father or to Pratibha. I hadn't said anything to my parents about her. I was totally foxed and bewildered. I took a long breath to regain my senses. I could hardly sleep that night. When I got up in the morning, I decided to write to my father about Pratibha. Actually same day, I sent a letter to my father. I and Pratibha started spending more time together. Hardly 10 days were left to leave the academy, when Prathibha told me, 'Raj! I thought I must tell you something about my past to avoid any stress in our future relationship.'

'What's that?' I curiously enquired.

'I was in a relationship with one of my classmate in college days. He broke relationship to go to the USA for his higher studies. I was unwilling to go along with him, as I wanted to remain in my own country,' she confided with me.

'So what? In college days, I was also having a relationship,' I said. 'There's nothing unusual about it. Albeit it's good, you told me all this to lighten your mind. I don't think it would've impacted our relationship in any manner, even if you haven't mentioned about it to me.'

'I must confess, it was something more than just being a friend,' Pratibha further confided. 'We're in love and wanted to marry. It was unfortunate that he decided to migrate. He persuaded me to accompany him to the USA. However, I preferred to remain in this country, instead of going with him in search of a greener pasture.'

I was shocked to hear all this. I told her, 'I'm also interested in going abroad. I might leave this job, if I get some good opening either in the USA or UK.'

'I must clarify that if you've any intention to settle abroad, you should forget me. I've no intention to migrate to any foreign country,' she said very emphatically.

'What're you talking about? Do you want to break our relation on this ground only?' I questioned her.

'I've no intention to break relationship, unless you desist from harboring the idea of settling in any foreign country,' she said firmly.

'I must be honest in confessing that it'd been my childhood dream to settle abroad. Many of my relatives are already settled either in the USA or UK. So, given an opportunity, I would love to migrate.' I reiterated my desire to settle in some foreign land.

'I don't think we're destined to live and grow old together. You just forget me,' she said and left me.

That very incident really shattered me and after that we started distancing from each other. Every passing day had widened our relations and finally we left for our respective postings. Thus, our marriage never took place,' explained Raj about his inability to marry his soul mate.

'Trine-Trine,' call bell again rang.

'It must be a waiter. Raj! Please open the door,' I requested him.

Raj got up and went to open the door. It was the same waiter, who came to serve us coffee.

'Coffee please. May I serve you?' Asked the waiter.

'Yes, you can,' said Raj.

The waiter placed his tray on the table and gently lifted cattle to serve coffee. He started pouring coffee in the cup, while asking, 'How much sugar Sir-one or two cubes?'

'No sugar for me,' I said.

'I'll prefer one. You just put sugar and give me the cup to stir,' said Raj.

'Do you need anything else? Asked the waiter politely.

'Thanks, you may go now,' said Raj to permit the waiter to leave the room.

The waiter left the room and Raj got up to close the door. After closing the door, he came back and sat on his chair. He lifted his cup and started mixing sugar.

'You told me that you'd written to your Dad about your relationship with Pratibha. What was his response?' I enquired from Raj.

While sipping his coffee, Raj said meditating, 'My Dad had been a very liberal person. He accepted graciously our relationship by sending me his consent through return mail. He was really hurt, when I told him that we weren't getting married and had broken our relationship.'

'So, you got engaged with Teena after your breakup with Pratibh,' I probed Raj, while seeing through his eyes in search of the truth.

'I refused to marry Teena and went to Chennai for taking up my new assignment,' said Raj. 'I was really hurt and wanted some time to heal up and forget Pratibha. However, my father was very adamant to get me married as early as possible. One day, my father came to my place along with his friend and Teena. She was a tall, slim and good looking girl. They spent two days with me. It gave me an opportunity to chat with Teena and know her. She was doing her post-graduation in economics from Cambridge University and wanted to pursue her career in the private sector. I'd no issue with that. Her father was working in the Commonwealth Secretariat. I thought, he may be, having good links and can be instrumental in getting me deputed either to Commonwealth or Asian Development Bank. Neither I had discussed with Teena about her career plan in detail, nor did I inform her about my intention to work in the UK, which turned out to be a big folly on my part. We got married and were blessed with a daughter in a year's time. Our relations, however, became bitter instead of gaining warmth. I wasn't very comfortable with Teena. I may share with you just two incidents, which didn't allow us to remain together. And, we landed in a court of law to seek a divorce in less than two years after our marriage.'

He again sipped his coffee and took a long breath before further telling me his story.

'Jai! You know, human being is a very complex animal. Everyone thinks, he's the only wisest person in this world and rest are fools. In his view, all can commit mistakes except him. You used to tell me, 'If you've premarital relations, you're bound to compare your wife with all yours Ex(s),' and on this issue I used to fight with you…'

I couldn't hold my curiosity to ask him, 'Why're you getting so emotional and philosophical? Do you rue your conduct?'

'Will you mind to have patience?' Raj said, while gazing at me.

'Please continue with your narration.' I quietly yielded to his request.

'Things happened exactly as per your prognosis about my marital life. I used to compare Teena with my all other girlfriends and would find some fault in her to quarrel. Wittingly or unwittingly, I'd say something that would hurt her and land us in fighting with each other. One summer evening, I came from the office and wanted to have a quick shower because the weather was warm and sultry. I got undressed and wrapped myself in a bath towel to take shower. Teena came and saw me in that dress and said very mischievously, 'Darling! You look very sexy in this costume.'

I looked at her, she was rigged in her skirt and top. I responded, 'If I look sexy in this dress, you aren't less foxy in your skirt.'

She gave me a very naughty look and tried to pull my towel. I held her hand and pulled her closer to me. I tried to pull her skirt. In this game we didn't know when we landed on our bed and spend good time in consummating our marital bliss. Suddenly, she said, 'Raj! You know, today for the first time, I've really very satisfying sex with you.'

'What do you mean to say, 'for the first time, I had very satisfying sex with you? Have you not had satisfied sex with me in the past?' I questioned her.

'I have had, but not as joyful as I've today. In the past, we'd had sex just like any other married couple might have.'

'How do you know about sex life of other married persons?'

'My friends tell me and you yourself must be knowing about it. Most of the people are boring in sex. They'll be over in five minutes. They don't know how to enjoy it.'

'It means you've enjoyed sex before marriage and know what's good or bad sex.'

'Why're you making it so personal? Everyone knows, you had relations with many girls before marrying me. So, what did you expect from me. I shouldn't have any boyfriend. If you can befriend girls and break your relations after enjoying them,

I can also do that. Don't you think your ex-girlfriends may marry some other persons in their life? Would they forget their past, when they marry with someone in the later part of their life? Never. Neither men, nor women can forget their past. So don't debate over such things, which're so obvious,' Teena said all this a bit rudely and sarcastically.

'Since then our relations lost the lustre and warmth. Whenever I made love with her, I thought about her alleged past relations. I started visualising her with different guys in different compromising positions. I lost my nerve and peace. Our relations got blown up, when I asked her father to help me in getting migrated to the U.K. Teena confronted me, 'You know, why I married you? I wanted to settle in India and not in the UK. Had I've any intention to settle in the UK, I would've married with any British Citizen. I thought you were in government service and would remain in India, so I agreed to marry you. Now you want to migrate to the UK. It wouldn't be possible for you to go out of India without divorcing me.'

'I was shocked to hear this. It took me some time to regain my senses. Since that day, we didn't have normal relations and finally we got mutually divorced within six months. She took my daughter. I agreed to that, as my daughter was very young and I was unable to look after her,' said Raj, very remorsefully to explain his agony.

'So, your past Karma is still haunting you. It's your past licentious libertine lifestyle, which compelled you to compare Teena with other women. You started suspecting her. Certainly, it wasn't right on your part to visualise her sleeping with other guys. Since you yourself enjoyed sex before marriage, you thought same about Teena. I don't know how you can think of marrying a virgin girl, when you yourself, being prurient and licentious, had enjoyed sex with several women in your life before marriage. Since one can't marry with each girl he befriends, it's likely that he gets a spouse having equal lust for premarital relations. Thus, in such promiscuous and consumerist environment, chances of getting a virgin girl as a spouse remain very low. That person can be you…'

Raj was getting restless, so interrupting me he said, 'We all know this. But, irony of life is that every man in his heart cherishes a wish of getting married with a virgin girl.'

'You're right. However, you can't negate the reality of life. It's not possible to have a cake and eat too,' I replied.

Raj got up and opened a water bottle and poured the water in a glass to drink. He again started telling his story, while sipping the water from his glass.

'You know, I didn't marry for almost three years after divorcing Teena,' said Raj. 'Second time, I decided to marry with a simple girl hailing from a small town. I thought, a girl from small town might be free from all ills of a big city. I forgot, life wasn't one dimensional. In big cities, life has its own challenges to meet with, which're different from that of a small city. I didn't realise, it might be difficult for a small city girl to adopt the lifestyle of a metropolis.'

'You're right,' I simply responded.

'Once I'd gone to Ludhiana for meeting my uncle, who enquired about my plan for second marriage. I briefed him about the girl, I was looking for as my spouse. He mentioned about Sushma and her family. Sushma was born and brought up in a small town of Ludhiana city, where her parents were doing some business. She graduated from one of the Ludhiana colleges. I find her meeting my criteria of a simple girl, so I agreed to meet her. The next day my relatives organized our meeting. At that time, I'd no expectation from my life. So,

I met Sushma and consented to marry her in a very simple ceremony. Some of my relatives dissuaded me from marrying her in a haste. They advised that Sushma was too simple to adjust to my lifestyle. I didn't listen to their advice and finally got married to Sushma,' said Raj.

'So, you must be very happy with Sushma, as she hails from a small town of Punjab,' I commented.

'Please keep on listening and make no comments. I'll tell you everything, but have patience. Hardly three months passed after my marriage with Sushma, I realized that I'd made another blunder in my life. Now I'd to repent for my folly. Sushma was really a too simple girl to adjust with me. She'd never visited any five star hotel or clubs in her life. One day, we'd gone to an Officer's club to attend a party. One of my colleague offered to shake hands with her and she politely greeted him with 'Namaste.' Someone offered her wine, she refused. And when he tried to hold her hand to dance with, she slapped him. It was a scene. Somehow, I managed the situation. I was very unhappy about her conduct. Next day, I consulted with one of my colleague to fix some tutor, who could coach her about all etiquette and manners of different parties and occasions. I arranged cookery classes for her, but due to my stupidity, she was in pup within a month's time. This incapacitated her to attend her cookery classes and other domestic works. It was another mistake on my part to neglect her physical condition and expect her to groom herself for new life. In due course of time, she delivered a baby girl. She got busy with her new happiness and started neglecting me. Gradually her warmth vanished and she became very dry. She lost interest in everything, but for household affairs and her baby. After two years, we're blessed with a son. Now she had one more person to look after. Her children and house became focal point of her attention. She was unwilling to accompany me in any party and preferred to stay in home.

She'd been reluctant to dine out or go out for entertainment. I started devoting most of my time to official works and go home just to sleep. Thus we became almost antisocial among friends and relatives. Our relationship became burdensome. I stopped inviting people to my home. We're actually living, as strangers under one roof, despite being husband and wife in public eyes. This's the reason, I lost touch with you also,' said Raj to confide with me about his sufferings. His remorse filled face was a clear testimony of his guilt and agony.

'Don't lose your heart. God's great, he may help you,' I said consoling him.

'I need to atone my sins,' he said with a big sense of relief.

'Raj, your talk reveals that in your first marriage, there was a lack of trust. Actually, trust is the lifeline of every relationship and particularly for marriage. If there isn't any trust between husband and wife, there is no free flow of emotions and consequently no emotional bonding between them. Until your partner feels emotionally secured with you, she wouldn't open up her heart to share her happiness, sorrow, hurt, pain and pleasure with you…'

'It's easy to preach than practice. How can you trust your spouse, once you know her past? It isn't easy to trust anyone,' Raj said, while interrupting me. His facial expression was clearly betraying a sign of friendly anger and frustration.

'You may be right. But you've to forget your past to lead a new happy life. You should realise that till you don't secure your partner emotionally, love can't flourish. This doesn't happen till your spouse feels that she'll be loved in all conditions, whether you know her past or not. If your wife is confident that none of her past misdeeds are going to lower her status and she would continue to be your darling, she'll be emotionally secured. This assurance is the key of a happy union and healthy married life. Your suspicious nature might've destroyed the very foundation of your marital bliss, which can bloom only through the trust. And once relationship is broken, it can only lead to closure of hearts and snapping of the communication, which puts last nail in the coffin of dead relations,' I said to make a philosophical observation.

'Jai, it appears you're right,' said Raj. He paused for a moment. A sign of trepidation was clearly visible on his face. He again started speaking, looking at the roof as if he was recollecting something. 'I hardly used to communicate with her and spent most of the time in office or in the tour. Perhaps, this uncaring attitude didn't allow her to trust me.'

'Your indifferent attitude might've stifled the flame of love in your relationship and she might've also stopped communicating with you,' I said considering myself as a great psychologist. 'Raj, do you know that one has to endeavor hard to close the heart and communication? A normal human being loves to talk, which's the distinguishing characteristic of human being from the rest of the animal world. If you snap communication, it works as a slow poison to your happy relationship. You mayn't realise, when your vibrant, happy life becomes a dead wood. So never break communication in any relation, particularly in married life,' I said to further explain my observations about his conduct towards his wife.

'Perhaps, you may be right. My yearning for migration and past love lingering became the potential cause of conflict. We started fighting frequently on some or other issue and...' Raj gasped his last words.

'In any relationship, difference and conflicts are bound to occur, as two persons can't have always the same thoughts, attitude, desires and expectations. If there isn't any conflict in a relation, it means parties are either not in talking terms, or they've hardened hearts. This may work for some time, but not in the long runs. Conflicts must be managed in time. Couples face the risk of divorce, if they don't work out their differences and manage their conflicting issues in time...'

Interrupting me, Raj said, 'I feared confrontation, lest it should spoil our relationship. So, I chose to buy peace at any cost and tried to sweep all conflicting issues under the rug. Most of us do it to buy peace at home, as I did by avoiding talks with my wife. Now in retrospection, I can say that this strategy doesn't pay in a long run. Suppressed conflicts remain buried alive, and may burst suddenly like a volcano, leaving your family devastated and frustrated.'

Defending himself, Raj further said, 'I agree, one shouldn't stop communication. But, I couldn't help myself. You know I'm not alone in this game. Most people, for a good reason, view conflict as a negative thing having potential to spoil the family peace. They believe that the arguments and angry interactions between a husband and wife aren't just stressful, but also unhealthy. So like others, I never tried to confront with Sushma or tried to manage any conflict with her.'

'It's very unfortunate to consider conflict as a negative thing,' I said. 'On the contrary, it provides you an opportunity to solve your issues to prevent their recurrence. Actually conflict is part of any relationship, including marriage, and it needs to be managed in a healthy way. It's pertinent to understand that conflict is to be managed and not resolved. If the conflict is managed by understanding each other's point of view, it leads to strengthening of the marital relations. If conflict is resolved, it may give temporary peace and mayn't lead to deepening of relations between the couple. Tone, language and words play a vital role in managing a conflict, so one should pay heed to all these nuances.'

Raj, expressing his anger, asked me in a bit of harsh tone, 'Please tell me how I should've managed the issue of migration.'

Without getting provoked, I explained, 'You should've confided Teena that you're desirous of taking some foreign deputation, while assuring her that you would come back to India, if she wasn't happy there. Or, you should've taken pain to understand the very cause of her resistance to migration and acted accordingly. Similarly, you should've spoken about her conduct, which was hurting you, instead of neglecting her. Your frank discussion might've given her an opportunity to mend her behaviour to satisfy your ego or expectations. On the contrary, you just neglected her and gave her no opportunity to know you better and mend herself according to your wishes. Thus, non-communication didn't allow both of you to understand each other, leading to a disastrous married life.'

'How can you say so authentically that non-communication led to the dissolution of my marriage?' Raj questioned my observation.

'Non communication hardens your attitude with every passing day and makes it difficult for you to have normal relations. The ability to empathise also diminishes and you stop feeling pain and pleasure for your partner. And sometimes, you may feel like running away from the sight of a person you aren't speaking with,' I explained.

'I see your point. I didn't try to manage conflicting issues bothering us. On the contrary, I tried to avoid conflict to assuage Teena's feelings and that didn't work,' said Raj, exhibiting his frustration.

'In resolving conflicts, words, language, tone of the voice and body language play a vital role. If you're really serious and honest in addressing a conflicting issue for having family peace, you shouldn't hesitate in accepting your mistake. There shouldn't be an issue of who is winning and who is losing. The family pride and honour are protected by your unity and not by your capacity to win over your partner. Exhibition of self-pride in family relations is cancerous for healthy married life and is bound to destroy a marriage, whereas humility and compassion have the potential to cement marital ties. However, I think humility of one partner shouldn't be construed as weakness by other partner to make him or her yield under pressure,' I said.

'What you say appears to be rational. However, I fail to understand that many people leave their homes to work at faraway places and meet their spouses just once or twice in a year, and their marriages aren't dissolved. We lived together for two years under one roof, but got separated,' Raj expressed his bewilderment.

'No doubt, people migrate for work and live separated, far away from their homes, but their marriages survive. Do you know, why? Their spouses know that their partners haven't deserted them, but have gone away for earning livelihood, much needed for their survival. Unlike you, their emotional card isn't snapped. In your case, there wasn't any emotional connect, needed to maintain family unity. On the contrary, you acted as a stranger to each other, despite living together under one roof,' I explained.

'I see your point. I think, I lacked compassion which is, perhaps, the first step to move from an unhealthy conflict to intimacy. I failed to assuage her hurt feelings to create an emotional bonding,' said Raj.

'You've perfectly touched the right issue. As a compassionate spouse, you might've soothed her hurt feelings to vanish all her grievances in thin air. If compassion balm is applied immediately, rather allowing time to fly with hurt emotions, chances of normal relations getting restored are bright. I think, you also neglected your second wife, as she wasn't conforming to your expectation. And in turn, she responded with her indifference to make your life hell,' I said.

'I may fully agree with you,' said Raj. 'Over a period of time, it became practically impossible for me to bear the sight of Sushma. I dreaded her and tried to remain most of the time away from home. Albeit she tried to keep me in good humour, somehow all her attempts to appease me used to further annoy. Thus, with every passing day, our relations deteriorated. Nevertheless, we continued to remain in the wedlock for the sake of our children.' Raj explained his compulsion to live with Sushma.

'You decided to drag your relations for the welfare of your children. Many people do so. However, you must be knowing that unhappy couples adversely impact healthy grooming of their children,' I said. And changing the topic, I enquired, 'what are your children doing, Raj?

'My son is doing engineering from IIT Delhi and daughter is studying medicine,' said Raj.

'Great! Wish both of your children to have a very satisfying and prosperous career. What is their thinking about marriage?' I further enquired.

'Both are reluctant to marry, after seeing my plight,' said Raj.

'It's appreciable that your traumatic married life might've adversely impacted their thought process in their impressionable age,' I observed. 'The childhood agony of seeing their parents in an unhealthy marital relationship might be a potential cause of their aversion to marry.'

'You know what my son thinks about marriage?' He posed a question and without waiting for my reply, he said, 'Why should anyone get married and take lifelong responsibility of a person just for a few minutes pleasures, if one can have all the fun of life without undergoing the ordeal of a married life? He considers having 'live-in-relation' with any girl is the best substitute of a marriage, which has more pain than pleasure.' Raj apprised about his son's perception of the marriage.

'I'm not surprised to listen his views about the marriage. He echoes what you used to say about the marriage during your college days. History is repeating itself,' I said very coolly.

'You're again slighting me,' Raj said angrily.

'Not at all. Don't you think what I said is factually correct? You may recall our last conversation about your dilly-dally with different girls in college. I warned you that one day you might rue for being a wanton creature. Your son is mirroring your own life's philosophy and nothing else,' I tried to be logical to him.

'Jai! Don't you think you're too harsh to me? I hadn't cherished such ideology in my life. I'd always respected my female friends and colleagues. I never tried to take any advantage of them,' said Raj to convince me, while exhibiting some sign of anger on his face.

'Leave it. Tell me why your daughter is against marriage?' I probed.

'She thinks all men, like her father, hardly love and care for their spouse. So, why should she take all pain of getting married, if she can be happy otherwise? She thinks marriage institution is a part of the patriarchal system, designed by the male dominated society to enslave women for their labour and sexuality. Women lose their identity and freedom after marriage. Married women aren't even credited for their domestic labour and treated as a bonded workers. They're supposed to attend domestic works and produce male progeny for inheriting husband's wealth and keeping his family's name alive. So, why should she, as an educated person, patronise such an inequitable institution?' Raj said.

'I mayn't fully disagree with her. It's a fact that society does have gender biases. However, notwithstanding oppressive customs, enlightened families do give respect to their women and they're treated at par with their male folks. I can only say such lofty ideas sometime create an illusion of pursuing a right course in life. As time passes, you may feel lonely and then have a longing for a company. But, you won't get any company, as most of the people of your age are already settled. Chances of getting a good match are pretty high when you're in your twenties or early thirties. And after that, options start diminishing with every passing day,' I said and lifted a copy of the newspaper from the table to give it to Raj.

'Raj! May I request you to read this article, regarding delayed marriage? Though this article highlights cause of delayed marriage in America, it may've some relevance to our country as well. You read it yourself,' I said, while handing over him a copy of the Economic Times.

Raj took the newspaper from me and started reading it. "Twenty percent of adults older than 25, about 42 million people, have never married, up from 9% in 1960, according to data in a Pew Research Centre report published on 24.9.2014 (Wednesday). Since 1970, each group of young adults has been less likely to marry than the previous generation. Although part of the trend can be attributed to the fact that people are simply marrying older, Pew projects that a quarter of today's young adults will have never married by 2030, which would be the highest share in modern history. So left and right debate the relationship among marriage, parenthood and poverty, young people seems to be sending policy makers a message: Marriage is not necessarily part of their plan. That shift could reshape not just US families, but also policy on taxes, children and entitlement.

In many ways, the retreat from marriage is the result of evolving gender roles. But the decline is also a result of America's deepening socio-economic divide. Until a few decades ago, marriage was mostly an economic equation: Men earned money to support a family while women ran the household. But with the rise of birth control, household technology and women in the workplace, marriage became less about economics and more about love, as the social historian Stephanie Coontz described in her book, Marriage, a History: How love conquered Marriage. 'If you go back a generation or two, the couple would likely take the plunge together and build up their finance and nest egg together,' said Kin Parker, director of social trend research at Pew. "Now it seems to be this attitude among young adults to build up households before they get married."

Raj puts the newspaper back on the table and said, 'No doubt, the findings of the said research are pointing to a trend of evolving human relations in American society, but I think it's quite true about Indian society too.'

'Do you remember Raj, at what age you got married?' I enquired from Raj meditating over his story and the news report.

'How can I forget it? I met Pratibha when I was 24 years old, a charming and handsome young man. I was bowled over by her beauty at the very first encounter with her in a party. Since then I couldn't think of anything else except how to marry her.

In two-three meetings, I charmed her and soon she became my girlfriend. You know, we both loved each other very intimately, but I couldn't marry her despite my strong longing. Having known my desire to migrate, Pratibha refused to marry me. And then, I got married with Teena as per my father's wishes. That time, I was 26 years old,' Raj told me.

'Raj! Moral of the story is that everyone, like you, has some reason to marry,' I said. 'Perhaps your son and daughter are still too young and unsure of taking parental responsibilities. So you shouldn't worry much for their marriage.'

'You know, unlike Europeans, we Indian parents don't live for ourselves. We've two biggest worries in our life: Education and marriage of our children. We get lost in meeting mundane and humdrum day to day challenges of life. We don't enjoy our life like western people do. Our major part of the life is wasted on worrying about the wellbeing of our children. This creates tension in our married life, but we hardly accept this. And paradoxically, many of us will not hesitate in attributing their miseries to their children whose welfare is their prime concern. That's why India is incredible,' said Raj.

'No doubt, Indian society revolves around children. Over protection of the children sometimes obstruct their healthy growth. On the contrary, European society ensures their children, on attaining their adulthood, live their own life outside the family shelter. And perhaps, this provides them an opportunity to risk and innovate. That's why American and European countries are the leaders in innovations in every walk of life. However, your children are educated and intelligent, I don't think their marriage should be any botheration for you,' I commented.

'Jai! You don't realize, it's the society which bothers you. Inquisitions of relatives and friends about children's marriage make your life miserable. You're often greeted with their standard queries, 'when's your daughter getting married? I'm waiting for a big party. Hope you won't forget to invite us.' Raj halted his narration, as my phone started ringing.

'Trine-trine,' rang my phone. I saw, it was a call from my wife-Zoya.

'Hello, how're you?' Asked my wife.

'I'm fine.'

'When're you coming back?'

'I may leave Mussorie tomorrow evening to catch a night train from Dehradun to Delhi, and next day, by evening flight I should be back home,' I informed Zoya about my itinerary.

'Have you met with your old friends? I hope all of you must be having a gala time. Have you taken your lunch?' My wife enquired.

'Oh yes! I'd lunch with some of my friends, followed by a long chat for dessert. I'm sure, you must be enjoying your freedom and have no botheration of feeding your husband,' I jested.

'Are you pulling my leg?' She said.

'Can I dare to do so?' I politely replied.

'I know what you can do. I'm putting off my phone. Give me a ring when you board your flight for Mumbai, so that I can send the driver to pick you up,' she said and ended her call.

'Jai! Your conversation with your wife gives me an impression that she has a concern for you,' enquired Raj.

'Raj! You're right. Sometimes, she's too obsessed and sometimes she may even forget whether I exist. But, one thing is sure that she's very much concerned about my welfare,' I said.

'Lucky guy!' Said Raj, while lifting his glass to drink water.

'You know Raj! Every coin has two faces. You've seen one side and not the other one. You can't find a single person who's perfect. So when two imperfect people marry, it's their obligation to complement each other for creating synergy by converting their weaknesses into their strength. If any spouse tries to prove his or her superiority over other partner, you can take it granted that their life is destined to be hell,' I said.

'Jai, you're sounding like a spiritual Guru. It's easy to preach than practice. You tell me how you could manage your darling to have a happy married life,' Raj enquired from me.

'Raj, I'll let you know everything, but first tell me why does anyone marry?' I asked.

'I think- physical attraction, romantic emotions, longing for a company of opposite sex and mating requirement leading to sexual intimacy are some of the factors causing two individuals to enter into a wedlock,' Raj attempted to list reasons for a marriage.

'Really impressed! Your causal description for getting married appears flawless,' I said. 'Like any young man, I too had a longing for a perfect darling during my transition from adolescence to adulthood. My story matches with your reasons for marriage.'

'I'm interested to know your experience of marriage rather than listening my admiration for listing out the reasons to marry,' said Raj, while showing no interest in my compliment.

'I'll certainly confide you. Wait a moment. Let me drink water before I start telling you my story,' I said and got up to drink water. When I was pouring water in to a glass, I observed Raj was getting restless. I drank water and sat down on a sofa lying in front of Raj.

I saw my watch, it was 7.45 p.m.

'What about dinner, Raj? It is 7.45, others may reach the dining hall in next 15 minutes.

'I'm not interested in dinner. You may go, if you wish so.

'Why? Are you not hungry?'

'I'm feeling full, we haven't moved anywhere after lunch.'

'Okay, let's forget about dinner.'

'You tell me your story.'

I started telling him my story of the search for a perfect partner, while stretching my legs.

'I think the attraction for opposite sex starts sprouting in any human being from the very early age. When I was in a fourth standard, I'd liking for my principle's daughter, who happened to my classmate. Later on when I moved to another school, I became very friendly to my one of the classmate, who used to share her food with me. Once I refused to eat with her, she cried a lot. I lost her company due to the sudden transfer of her father. Similarly, I was very much infatuated with my neighbour, who was in 7th standard. We're studying in different schools. We got separated within a year, as my father got transferred and we all had to move out along with him. This time, I really felt very bad about the transfer. I'd a hurt feeling to leave the said place. That fateful day, when we're to leave, she gave me her ring and said, "Keep my ring with you. It'll remind you about our friendship. Never forget me." I never realised how deeply she' was in love with me. It was almost 10 years later, when I got her message that she still remembers me and wanted to see me. Suddenly her last word echoed "never forget me" and I felt the chilling effect in my spine. However, I couldn't gather enough courage to respond her message, as I'd already moved on long back, almost forgetting her...'

'You mean to say that you never met her after leaving that place,' Raj, asked, while interrupting me. 'How come you didn't respond her message?'

'You know Raj. Actually, my search for my darling began the day my mother expressed her desire to see me married to get Bahu (daughter in law). One day, she called me and while showing a painting, said, 'I want you to marry a beautiful girl like this. I expect your wife to be well cultured, caring and compassionate human being.' All this she said when I was studying law and preparing for my various competitive exams for getting some good job.

'What're you talking Mom? I've no intention to marry till I'm settled. I'm still studying. You shouldn't talk to me about marriage at this stage,' I expressed my reservations.

'Why're you getting irritated? I'm not saying you get married right now. I'm just expressing my desire, how your wife and my 'Bahu' should look like,' said my Mom.

'That conversation sowed seeds of my longing for an ideal wife. I hadn't thought about my life partner before that incident, but since then whenever I saw any beautiful girl I used to evaluate the possibility of finding my soul mate. That yearning for an ideal soul mate guided my romantic journey. I started looking for female friends. In this adventure, access, proximity and what you say- looks played a dominant role. You tend to get attracted to people who're around you and easily accessible. I developed a friendship with my neighbour-Roni, who was a beautiful, intelligent and very studious girl. The other one was Mamta, who was my classmate. My infatuation with both of them was short lived and our relations ended abruptly,' I said.

'How come you aborted your friendship with both the girls at the same time?' Raj enquired.

'It was just a matter of chance and not a deliberate attempt. One evening, I was coming from the market and as I turned towards my house, I encountered with Roni. She was standing at her entrance gate. She stopped me and started chatting. She wanted me to spend some time with her. I was in a hurry to reach home to hand over the shopping bag to my Mom, who was waiting for me. Anyhow, she allowed me to go home after taking a promise for quick return to have evening tea with her. I promised and left for my house. I returned back to Roni's place after handing over the shopping bag to my mother. Incidentally, it was a very nice and pleasant evening of early winter. When I reached her house and pressed the doorbell, she opened the door in a moment. I was captivated seeing her in a stylish pink shirt and black slacks. She'd changed her previous dress. She was looking very gorgeous and charming in her new attire. 'You're stunning. Today you can kill anybody,' I said spontaneously.

'Will you come inside or remain standing outside only. You're behaving unlike Jai, who hardly appreciates anybody,' she said, while inviting me inside her house.

'I'm seeing you in such an attire for the first time. In this fitting, you're really looking terrific,' I said to admire her outfit, while entering her house.

I reached her drawing room and it appeared no one else was in her house. I asked her, 'Where's your Mom?'

'She's gone to meet her friend and may be back any time. What'll you like to have in snacks along with tea? I can fry something for you,' Roni gave me options to choose snacks, while answering my query.

'Thanks, I'll just love to take tea,' I said and started flicking through a magazine lying on the table. She left the drawing room to make tea. After a few moments, she came back with tea and snacks.

'You're so quick in doing all this. I hope it must be tasty too,' I complemented her, while expressing my surprise.

'Don't worry, you'll get a good tea. I'm sure you'll love it. Actually, I'd kept water on burner to make tea, as you promised to come back soon,' said Roni.

'Very smart…'

Interrupting me, she said, 'Don't flatter me. First taste the tea and then comment.' And she started pouring tea in a cup for me.

'May I help you? I tried to take the kettle from her hand. But she resisted. 'Let me have the pleasure of serving you. You're hardly seen in my house,' she commented and continued pouring tea in the cup.

'How much sugar do you want? One cube or two,' she enquired very affectionately.

'I think one sugar cube may be more than required, as your hands have already sweeten it,' I said flattering her.

'What do you think, I'll get flattered with such a silly remark?' She said, while smiling and twitching her lower lip. She kept on stirring the tea to mix sugar.

'How can any sensible person like me prevent himself flattering a beautiful girl like you, who cares so much for me? And if you've any reservation, I may like to withdraw my comments, Her Highness,' I said looking in her eyes.

'Hello. I don't bite,' she said, while handing over cup to me.

'But, I love a bite,' I said and tried to take a piece of snacks kept on the table. She laughed. 'Very smart. You'll love it also,' she said, while passing over snacks to me.

'Certainly. Since you've made, it's to be tasty,' I said and took snacks from her hand. While sipping the tea, I commented, 'Roni you've made very tasty snacks. Do you really love cooking or aunt has made it?'

'I've made it, just a few minutes ago. I love cooking,' she said enthusiastically.

'I'm sorry for asking such a stupid question, as most girls don't like to enter into the kitchen. They take pride in their ignorance, while deriding those who love it,' I explained the reason for asking such a silly question.

'I don't know why people try to belittle cooking ability. I love it and may cook despite having servants,' she said very proudly.

'How do you get time for cooking, when your study demands lot of time? Or once you're at a job, don't you think it'll be very taxing?' I enquired further to know her real craze for cooking.

'You can always get time for what you want to do and may've excuses for that you hate to do. Everyone has to give priority to his different jobs and rest is time management,' she spoke very confidently and with clarity.

We chatted for some time and suddenly she asked, 'How's your friend Mamta?'

Her inquisition about Mamta really foxed me. I wasn't aware that she knew about her. Pretending my ignorance, I enquired, 'Who is Mamta you are talking about?'

'You know very well, who I'm talking about. I know, she's your best friend. She's studying with you,' Roni asserted.

'Okay. You're referring to my classmate Mamta. How do you know her?' I asked a counter question.

'Yes, I'm mentioning about your dear classmate. She was my senior in school. I also know you're her best friend. But you don't know her well. She isn't a good girl. She's many friends and may ditch you someday…'

Interrupting her, I said, 'It isn't good to talk ill about someone in her absence. It'll be nice, if we spend this beautiful evening to chat about something else.'

'You know, I've no intention to defame her. I just wanted to caution you, as I know her for a long time,' she tried to defend herself.

In the meantime, her mother came and she metamorphosed into a different person, a stranger. While entering into the drawing room, her mother asked me, 'Hello Jai. How're you? Hope everyone is fine in your family.'

'Oh yes. Everyone is hale and hearty,' I said.

'How come you aren't seen for a long time?' She asked me further.

'You know these days exams are going on, so I hardly get time for an outing. Today, Roni caught hold of me and pressed to spend some time with her,' I said.

Listing to my comments, Roni suddenly interrupted and said, 'Mom, I'd been waiting for you eagerly, I need to go out to see my friend- Konkana. I'm already late. Now, you look after Jai, I'm going,' she said and left her house.

'She pretended as if I was holding her hand and she'd no interest in spending time with me. That day I decided, I'm not going to see this girl again. That was my last meeting with her. After that incident, her mother invited me numerous time to visit her house, but it was her wasteful endeavour. In retrospection, I can say that loss of friendship was a result of my impulsiveness, not expected from a matured and rational person. Perhaps, I wasn't mature enough to appreciate her situation and her feelings for me,' I said.

'Didn't you meet her after that incident?' Raj asked, not believing me.

'There'd been a few occasions when I just saw her, while passing through her house, but hardly had any conversation with her except exchanging formal greetings,' I explained.

'What happened to Mamta?' Raj further probed.

'Similarly, loss of my friendship with Mamta was another example of my impulsiveness and judgmental reaction. I befriended her in my final year of graduation. We became good friends and started spending time together. After graduation, she joined another college for doing her masters and I joined university to do law. However, we continued to be good friends.

You know, proximity brings closeness, and provides opportunities to explore other person in a better way. When you spend more time together, you can't suppress your natural behaviour for a long time to appease the other individual. Sometimes you may hurt others, leading to a conflict. We started knowing each other's strength and weaknesses, likings and disliking. As happens in any relation, we started fighting with each other and sometimes my sister used to help us patch up our strained relations. Notwithstanding our shortcomings, our friendship became more romantic over a period of time, giving way to emotions beyond our friendship. However, things were destined differently.

We all know that trust is the core of all relations, what to say about friendship alone. It's the trust, which creates bonding and intimacy. If the trust is broken, either in reality or in perception, result is the same- a death of the relationship. Same thing happened to our friendship.

Once, we'd gone for a family outing after a patch-up of our sour relations. My sister snapped us together with her conventional camera. Those days, we didn't have a smart phone to take selfies. My sister sent photo-reel to the studio for its development and her brother collected all the photographs from the said studio. However, she informed me that all the photographs were lost in transit. It was very shocking and unbelievable, but I forgot that incident as an accident. However, one day, I could see all those photographs in her room. I enquired and pressed her to tell me the real story of the lost photos. She informed that her elder brother forced her to tell that story. He desired, those photographs shouldn't be given to me. That hurts me very badly. I said, 'If for some reasons, best known to your brother, it wasn't desirable to show me the photos, at least you shouldn't have lied me.' I rebuked and reprimanded her. She tried to explain, 'It wasn't my intention to mislead you or conceal from you. Believe me…' Interrupting her, I said, 'Intentions are best known from the conducts of a person. There's no machine to read human intentions. You didn't repose your confidence in me. I don't think, we can move forward anymore. Roni had rightly cautioned me about your true nature. It was I, who refused to believe her.'

'What'd Roni tell you about me?' She curiously asked.

'It's not my business to tell you, what she said or how I feel about you. Henceforth, if you could remain just a friend of mine that itself be a big thing,' I said very rudely and left her home. I didn't visit her home for six months. Her mother endeavoured to resolve our differences, but my hurt was too deep to assuage. In the meantime, I got a job in a company, which posted me down south of the country. I left my city. When I was in training, I came to know she got married. She might've hardly celebrated her second marriage anniversary and she'd to bear the pain of divorce. No doubt, I felt very sad for her misfortune. She remained in my contact for some time, but there was no warmth in our relation and gradually things slipped into oblivion.'

'It's very strange, you never told me about all this during college days,' Raj enquired, while breaking his silence.

'You know, I hardly shared my personal feelings with anyone. Things changed with the passage of time. Today, I can talk to you frankly,' I said.

'Anyhow, tell me, what lesson did you take?' Raj further enquired.

'The lesson was loud and clear. Once you know someone's weaknesses, you shouldn't exploit. On the contrary, you should help her to improve. Besides, you should provide some space to your partner for the growth of her individuality, so that she shouldn't feel stifled. Secondly, you shouldn't try to outsmart your spouse, if you want healthy relation. Thirdly, one should try to appreciate her situation and reasons for a particular behaviour. Mamta told me the story of the lost photographs on the insistence of her brother, who must be extra careful about the reputation of her sister. There was nothing wrong with it. I should've appreciated this. Anyhow, my relations became casualty of distrust and my judgmental attitude,' I explained.

'It's really very sad. Please tell me, if you had some other romantic adventures during your service?' Asked Raj.

'You know after college, I joined my first service in Chennai. There're about 35 officers, including 14 lady officers. One day all officers were taken to Pondicherry for a picnic. When we're coming back, one female officer-Sheshadri enquired, 'How come you remain so reserved and look unromantic? Girls are very keen to befriend you, but for your attitude, they don't dare to.'

'I'm really surprised to know this- Sheshadri. Did I ever show you my attitude or rough up with any of you. How can you say I'm uncouth or unromantic? You're an English literature student and you'd know very well there're many moods of romance. I'm not sure of which romance you're talking about,' I said, while pretending my ignorance.

'How's it possible that you don't have any girlfriend, despite being young and handsome? If you're a romantic person, you must be having someone in your life.' She enquired, while expressing her surprise.

'Having a girlfriend is the litmus test of being romantic, I never knew this. Why don't you become my girlfriend and make me instantly a romantic person?' I jested.

'Jai, common! You're pulling my leg,' she said very affectionately, while coiling herself in shyness. Her crinkled cheeks looked very charming.

Suddenly the vehicle stopped, as we'd reached to our destination, and so our conversation also ended. However, since that day, Shesadri started showing her inclination to befriend me, but it was very short lived. One day, we're watching a TV show after dinner. Suddenly, I commented about the actress singing and dancing, 'She looks very beautiful, voluptuous and seductive. I feel very attracted to her.' I could hardly finish my sentence. She started yelling, on hearing my comment, 'Corrupt people like you encourage such type of women.'

There were some other officers watching the TV, when she made this comment. Her remark infuriated me to retort back, 'How dare you called me corrupt? God has created beautiful things to be appreciated. Actually, it's your meanness, which prevents you from appreciating other beautiful women.'

Perhaps, she hadn't expected any retaliation form my side. Listening my unpalatable remark, she immediately left the TV room without any comment or protest. And with this our communication also stopped.'

'Jai, don't you think you'd been too harsh with her?' Raj commented.

'I agree with you. I hadn't intended to hurt her. But, that was a very impulsive response from both the sides. She shouldn't have passed such an insulting comment on me. It was her spontaneous feminist response, smacking of her jealousy and mine was the function of hurt male ego. Thus sprouting of a romantic relationship got nipped in the bud,' I said with a heavy heart.

'So, you didn't have any interaction with her after that incident?' Raj further enquired.

'We started avoiding each other and within a week were given different assignments, so we hardly got time to interact. In a month's time, I was sent to Nagpur, a city in central Indian and she was moved down south to Mysore in Karnataka. And it was an end of a very short lived fairy tale,' I said.

'Jai, what was your expectation from your darling?' Raj probed.

'My first consideration was that my partner should be compassionate and caring, who can appreciate my family bonding and hold them tenaciously. Initially, as per expectation of my mother, I used to think of a housewife- caring, affectionate and a loving person. However, after joining this service, I realised that choice of a house wife won't be a right one. This idea became stronger during my training as a civil servant, which entailed huge job-responsibilities and frequent travelling. I thought, it might be very unfair for an educated lady to kill her time sitting idle in home and waiting for her husband to come back, particularly in a nuclear family. I was also aware about the difficulties in getting both the persons posted in one place, particularly when both are employed in different services or otherwise. So, I became more interested in a professional girl rather than a serving one to have better adjustment,' I explained the reasons for marrying a professional woman.

'If your parents were looking for a housewife, how could you convince them for a working girl?' Raj probed further.

'I must say, I'm lucky to have parents who never tried to impose their likings and disliking on their children. We're given full freedom to choose our partners. When I explained them the reason for opting for a working girl, they happily agreed,' I told him.

'How'd you find your sweetheart? Was it a love tangle or gift of arranged marriage?' Raj enquired.

'I couldn't cherish an idea of seeing a girl in the presence of her parents and relatives. To me it looks like searching for a product in a place where a woman is presented as a commodity. And like other producers of goods, parents and relatives narrate the qualities of their girl to make you interested in marrying her. How can you decide about marriage in a meeting, lasting for a few minutes? Most of the time, decisions are taken on the basis of looks, family background and apparent traits, as informed by the respective parents or guardians of the woman. So, such relations sometimes works and sometimes don't…'

'That's the reason, I used to say, it's necessary to spend some time with a girl to know her true nature and possibility of having compatibility,' said Raj, while interrupting me. 'And you used to oppose my friendship with them.'

'No. I wasn't against your friendship with any girl.' I countered him. 'I didn't favour your licentious behaviour and flirting with every girl.'

'Okay, you tell me about your marriage,' Raj requested.

'I consider myself a lucky person, who got the better of both the worlds. Our marriage was a love-cum-arranged one. I used to transit through Delhi, while going to Mumbai. Once I happened to be in Delhi, I was invited for dinner by my friend- Rohan Shikhdhar. And there, incidentally, I met my darling Zoya. She was studying medicine and was at the verge of completing her MMBS. That was a very interesting evening. In just one hour time, I and Zoya became friends. Since then, whenever I visited Delhi in regard to my work or otherwise, we used to spend time together. We dated for a year.'

'Oh, you got Zoya in Delhi! Very strange. You didn't get anyone in Mumbai?' Raj commented.

'Are you interested in listening or would you investigate why I met her in Delhi?' I said.

'Please tell me your story. I just commented, please don't get offended.' Raj said.

'It was one of the Saturdays in autumn, when we went to Humayun Tomb. Where we encountered one of my old friends Shahil, who saw us siting and chatting on the lawn. He came close to us. 'Hi Jai! How're you? Have you got married? How come you didn't invite me?' He surprised us with a volley of his queries.

'Hi Shahil. How come you got the impression that I got married?' I responded quickly, while attempting to read Zoya's flustered facial expression; which betrayed her nervousness, as she started twisting her scarf.

'I'm not married. She's just my friend,' I said quickly to dispel his wrong impression.

'Shahil, Meet Zoya. She is my friend,'I said to introduce him to Zoya.

'Nice to meet you. I'm sorry for my stupidity,' said Shahil to greet her, while being apologetic for his wrong comments.

Having realized his mistake, Shahil was uncomfortable with Zoya and excused himself to leave us within a moment.

'Jai. I think I should move. I'll see you some other time,' he said and left us, without waiting for my response.

'I think, we should also go back,' said Zoya and started moving towards exit gate.

'Why should you change your mind? We're supposed to spend some time here. And now you want us to go back. You shouldn't feel bad about Shahil's remark. I don't know why people can't think beyond marriage, if they see a boy and girl together,' I said and held her hand to dissuade her from going back.

'No, I'm not feeling bad about his remark. But, I want to go back,' she said and actually moved, pulling her hand from my grip. I followed her. That day, she didn't take lunch with me and took a taxi for her hostel. I also left for my guest house. That incident spoiled our good mood. I went back to Mumbai next day. I again happened to visit Delhi on the very next Monday. I fixed up lunch with Zoya in United Cafe, a restaurant in Connaught place. We'd our lunch. And when we're getting down from the stairs, we met Mrs. Mehra, who happened to be her aunt's friend. She didn't say anything, except enquiring about her general well-being. 'Hi Zoya. How're you?'

'I'm fine,' said Zoya, while greeting her.

'Is he your friend?'

'Yes.'

I also wished her. With a small conversation with her, we left the restaurant.

On my next meeting, Zoya told me, 'Jai, do you recall our last meeting with Mrs. Mehra?'

'Of course.'

'She'd told my aunt about you. Now my aunt wants to meet you,' said Zoya.

'What's making your aunt to have an interest in me?' I questioned her.

'Nothing special. Actually, she's invited me for dinner and I wish you to join me,' she said very innocently.

'If she has invited you, you better go. I may meet some other friend tomorrow evening,' I said.

'I don't want to miss your company, so please come along with me,' she said to persuade me.

Anyhow, I accompanied Zoya for dinner to her aunt's house. Her aunt appeared to be a nice lady. Her husband and she met me very warmly and gave a good treat. Her aunt talked to me when Zoya went in another room with her cousins. 'What's your marriage plan?' Her aunt inquired.

'I haven't thought about it,' I said.

'Why?'

'I think marriage spoils good friendly relations. After marriage, each partner starts taking other for granted. She may've higher expectation from me than what she's today.'

'Is any other reason to avoid marriage?'

'Another reason is my impulsive behaviour. I can't bear with a casual approach in personal relations,' I said.

'Your friend is very methodical and cares for you. I think you shouldn't have any problem with her,' She said to convince me.

'You know, one can maintain good composer while meeting friends for a short span of time,' I said. 'But, can't have the same temperament all the time, when you start living together. Sometimes, you're in a bad mood and you don't respond as per other's expectations. Whereas your partner wants you to be humorous and courteous all the time, which isn't human. This leads to conflict and spoils relations. So, I want to remain just your friend.'

'This's a universal fact and despite this people marry. Marriage will bring stability in your relation. I think, you should consider her for marriage,' she said.

'Aunty let's have dinner, as I'm getting late,' said Zoya, who came to invite us for dinner.

After dinner, I went to my guest house and Zoya went to her place. We didn't have any time to discuss about what her aunt talked to me.

We used to discuss about our career plan, family, likings and disliking etc., but never talked about our marriage plan. It was a beautiful romantic Sunday in early winter, when Zoya enquired me about the future of our relations.

'Jai, we'd been meeting for last one year. Now, we know each other quite well. What do you think about the future of our relation? Will we be just a friend or can have some more lasting relationship?' Enquired Zoya.

I wasn't prepared for such a query. I got a bit nervous and didn't know what to say. Somehow, I responded, 'What do you know about me?'

'As far as I know, you're an intellectually honest and compassionate person. You respect women and care for me. You've a good job and may like to have a settled married life,' she said to explain her understanding about me.

'Do you think, I'm a perfect person for you and we can grow old together?' I asked her.

'No one is perfect including me. Everyone has some shortcomings. It's for us to make our relations perfect. I'm pretty sure that I would be delighted to get married to you and I love to grow old with you. But, I'm not sure what you feel about me,' she explained.

'You know, my greatest weakness is my impulsive nature, and when I'm angry, I don't know how to treat people. You mayn't be an exception and then you may repent your decision,' I hesitantly told her about my weakness.

'I know this. I also know that you're a very rational man and don't hesitate in accepting your mistake. You also feel sorry on realising your mistake and show your willingness to mend your conduct. This's yours the greatest strength. This gives me hope that our relationship can be lasting one,' she replied me very affectionately.

'You know, we come from different social and linguistic background. Our parents mayn't consent to our relationship. Generally, it's believed that people of the same language, religion and community make happy couples. So, it mayn't be easy for us to move forward and have good compatibility.' I expressed my hesitation in accepting her proposition.

'Do you think compatibility is a function of belonging to the same language, community and religion? Has it been true, there would've been no divorce amongst couples having the same religion, caste or language? I don't bother what others think. I certainly care for my parents' wishes and will marry you with their blessings only. I'm sure you may also like to do the same. Now, you let me know your mind and then talk about consent of the parents?' She emphatically demanded my immediate response.

'Your rationality and maturity of thought is certainly amazing. I'll be privileged to have you as my life partner. However, I must confess that I haven't given any thought about this in the past. So, please give me some time to think over it. I would let you know shortly about my decision,' I said and left the place hurriedly, before she could say anything.

On my way back to the guest house, I started a fresh musing over the entire conversation, I'd had with Zoya. I wasn't sure, whether Zoya had understood me completely. I knew, she'd ambition to pursue her higher studies in Delhi. I may or mayn't get posted in Delhi. An adjustment may be a big issue. I love good home food and she craves for dining out. If possible, she may dine out every day. I don't know, how my parents are going to react. I reached my guesthouse, while thinking all this, but couldn't arrive at any conclusion. Next day, I left for Mumbai. Hardly a month passed, when I had to visit my home. My parents wanted to discuss some issue relating to family business.

Next day, I was having evening tea with my parents. I found them in a very relaxed mood. I thought, it should be a right opportunity to raise Zoya issue with them.

'Dad, I want your permission to marry a Marathi girl, who's in her final year of MBBS. Her parents are also in the medical profession,' I asked my father, when my mother was pouring tea in his cup to serve him. Listening me, she stopped pouring tea.

'Are you serious? Do you really want to marry a girl out of our community?' He questioned.

'I won't allow you to marry any girl, who isn't from our community or from a different state,' was a curt reply from my mother.

Responding to my father's query, I said. 'The main issue is the choice of a girl with whom I can have compatibility. I know Zoya for the last one year and I think she should be the right choice for me. We can make a good couple…'

'I don't want to have a Marathi Bahu. She doesn't understand our culture and customs,' said my mother, interrupting me. 'What'll people say? I'm not going to allow you to marry her. You couldn't find any other girl in our own caste.'

'Mom, what is in the caste? It used to represent the person's profession, but now it's only an instrument of identity politics and nothing else, I said. 'Like millions of other people, I'm in government job instead of managing the family business. Today caste system serves no purpose, except to divide the society and prevent India from becoming one nation. Had our society, not been divided into numerous castes and sub-castes, it wouldn't have been possible for thousands of foreigners to enslave millions of Indians for hundreds of years.'

'You don't know how relatives will react? There may be a problem in your sister's marriage,' told my Mom to share her concern.

'I'm sure no sensible person of the family or society may oppose it. And if anyone does so, I don't care. They won't come to feed us, if we're starving. Self-proclaimed leaders may like to needle in other's personal affairs without shouldering corresponding responsibility of nurturing a family. You shouldn't bother about my sister, who's well educated to look after herself,' I said to counter her.

'I don't want to argue with you. I fear that a girl from different culture and practicing other customs mayn't find it easy to adjust with us,' told my Mom to express her fear.

'Ma! What's the guarantee that I'll have a smooth married life, if I marry a girl of our own community and she won't create any problem?' I said. 'You know, there's no dearth of people marrying within their own community and getting divorced. However, it also doesn't mean, I won't have any conflict in my marital life, if I marry Zoya. Some differences may always be there, whosoever I am married. There're occasions, when you don't agree with dad. Does it mean, you've bad marriage? No. You differ with dad, because you've different views on the subject. Belonging to the same community is no guarantee that my wife will understand me better or there won't be any differences between us. I only know, I may've better chances of marital compatibility with Zoya.' I explained my views about the consequences of marriage within or out of the community.

'Are you in serious love with Zoya?' Asked my father.

'I like her and think we can do well. I mayn't marry her, if you don't agree. However, you should know, I don't like to marry any girl just by seeing her face or on the tips of some of our relatives,' I said to put forth my views.

'Do you think her parents will also agree?' Asked my father.

'We won't marry till both the families approve our relationship, as marriage isn't just a union of two individuals, but also that of two families,' I said.

'Give us some time to think. I'll let you know before you leave,' said my father and left us.

'I wasn't expecting you to behave like this? I'm very angry with you,' said my mother.

'I assure you Ma, she'll keep you happy, not less than yours other Bahu,' I said emphatically holding her hand.

Next day, we're all having breakfast, when my Dad said, 'You should know, Jai wants to marry a Marathi doctor girl. We've no objection, if the girl's parents also agree to this relationship.'

Hearing this, my brother and sister started raising their objections. They weren't in agreement. The dining table turn into a mini parliament. Everyone was speaking except my parents, who were listening every one with full attention.

'Stop all the discussion. We've heard all of you,' said my father, abruptly. 'We've deliberated on the subject. The issue of marriage pertains to Jai. And, if he thinks, he can have a better life with Zoya, no one else should've any objection. It's for Jai to take a call, with full sense of responsibility, in his own interest and that of the family too.'

Thus the whole issue got halted. My siblings and some of my other relatives were very unhappy with me. However, they'd to reconcile.

Next day, I flew to Delhi to catch my evening flight to Mumbai. My flight reached Delhi at 10.30 a.m. and my Mumbai flight was at 6 p.m. There was sufficient time to spend with Zoya, who wasn't aware about my visit to Delhi. So after reaching guest house, I spoke to Zoya and invited her for lunch. Since I'd no other engagement, I sat down on the rocking chair and started deliberating over issues, I needed to discuss with Zoya.

My concentration was broken by the ring of the doorbell. I opened the door. As per my expectation, it was Zoya.

'Hi, how're you?' I passionately asked her, while hugging her.

'I'm fine. Hope you're having a good time,' said Zoya, while smiling, to respond my greeting.

'Please, take your chair,' I said.

'Thanks,' said she and pulled a chair to sit close to me.

I took the subject head on without losing any time, as I was scheduled to go to Mumbai by the evening flight.

'Zoya, last time you wanted to know about the future of our relationship,' I said to remind her about her inquisition. 'I promised you to respond during my next visit. I deliberated over it and thought: if I've to marry someone, why not you. You aren't a bad choice. I can tolerate you for the rest of my life.'

Hearing this, she lifted a magazine lying on the centre table and started hitting me affectionately.

'Stop it. What're you doing? If this's the beginning, what'll happen to me, once I get married to you?' I said, while holding her hand.

She pulled her hand and embraced me for a few seconds and then kissed me few times.

'I'm so happy, you can't imagine. Thanks God for hearing my prayers and fulfilling my wish. Now, I've to speak to my parents. I don't know, whether you've consulted your parents?' Zoya expressed her happiness.

'Actually, my parents wanted to discuss some business matter, so I had to visit my home. Today, I've come straight from my home. I took this opportunity to know their reaction to our marriage. I had discussed with them. Initially they refused, however, after some discussion and reasoning, they agreed to our marriage on a condition: your parents should approach them for our marriage. I've promised them, I won't marry you till your family agree to our marriage. I hope, you've no reservation,' I said to brief her about the reaction of my parents.

'I'm extremely happy to know this. I think, my parents should also agree to our marriage,' said Zoya, while hugging me again.

'Zoya! Albeit I agree to marry you, but there're some issues which need to be sorted out,' I said.

'What're those issues, which're bothering you? I think, all major issues have already been resolved,' she quizzed.

'You know, you're a pure vegetarian, but I'm not. You love dinning out and I prefer home food. You want to live in Delhi and my job requirement may take me to any part of the country. You don't believe in customs and my mother wants her Bahu to follow them religiously. These and some other divergence in habits and expectations may create differences between us. Right now, you won't consider them a big issue, but these things are bound to crop up to bother us in due course of time. If the same aren't taken in the right perspective to manage, we may've a big mess after marriage. I don't know, how're we going to treat them? If we aren't able to have some understanding right now about how to manage such issues, we should forget about marriage and better remain as friends. Unmanaged issues mayn't only spoil our marriage, but can also ruin our friendship. It's necessary to have some understanding right now to stave off the failings in our marriage. Otherwise, antagonist of love-marriage may unwittingly get a chance to buttress their stand against such relations,' I told her my apprehension about the possibility of having trouble in marital relations.

'I appreciate your apprehension. In fact, I too deliberated over some of these issues. Let me explain my point of view. No doubt, I'm strict vegetarian and would be happy, if my husband is also a vegetarian. I'm certainly not comfortable with non-veg food in my home. All other issues are manageable. However, you shouldn't accept this relation, if you can't live without non-veg food,' said Zoya to explain her point of view.

'It isn't the issue of just my choice of veg or non-veg food. What may happen, if friends or relatives come to our place for lunch or dinner and they desire non-veg food? Don't you think, it may embarrass us, if we refuse them?' I further probed.

'Most often, we ourselves are responsible for people's expectation, but we blame others,' she said. 'People don't expect you to serve non-veg food, once they know you're a vegetarian person. Similarly, if you don't like dinning out, I may also start liking home food. Today, I've no options, but to dine out; so I love it. These aren't all serious issues, which we can't manage.'

'What about your indifference to family customs and rituals?' I asked.

'I can manage all these things, you can be rest assured. You tell me what you want?' She posed a straight question to me.

'Have you spoken to your parents? What's their reaction?' I put a counter question.

'I haven't spoken to them so far. I wanted to know your view first, before I take up the issue with my family. I wanted to be sure of your decision, which matters to me the most. Now, I know your view as well as that of your parent's, so it'll be easy for me to speak with my parents. My parents are very liberal. I don't see they may've any objection, if I'm happy about it. The greatest worry of parents is that their daughter should get married to a well settled person, hailing from a good family. You're meeting all the criteria of a good groom, except that you aren't from our community. Though it may be a major issue in some families, but I don't think, it'll be a big issue in my family to prevent our marriage,' she said very confidently.

'Consent of your parents will not be a problem in our marriage, but my conscious says that our divergent job requirements, nature and habits may certainly pose a real threat to our marriage,' I said. 'So, I'm a bit concerned about it.'

'What do you think of me? Am I too immature to handle domestic affairs or incapable to check my whims and fancy to spoil our marriage?' She questioned me.

'I'm talking about myself and not about you. I know my impulsive nature, which may get triggered by some of your strong likings and disliking to rock our boat,' I said. 'Anyhow, if you think you can manage the probable conflicting issues, I'll be happy to marry you.'

'You don't sound very confident,' she observed and said further, 'It appears you doubt me. You must be thinking that I can't handle all the conflicting issues, you just mentioned. If you're still having some lingering doubts, I can wait for. I'm confident of myself and can't think of anyone else. But, you shouldn't take any decision, if you yourself aren't sure of it.'

'Let's take lunch. It's already 3 p.m. I've to catch my evening flight and for that I've to leave the guest house by 4. 30 p.m.' I said.

'Okay, let's start,' she said.

We started eating food and hardly spoke while eating lunch. Once we finished our lunch, she enquired, 'When can I expect you to give me your final answer?'

'I must accept, I'm a bit confused, I said. 'However, you can speak to your parents, I've no reservation to marry you.'

She hugged me and said, 'Thanks.'

We chatted for some time and after that, I left for the airport and she went to her hostel.

After a fortnight, I got a letter from Zoya to inform me about the concurrence of her parents. Same day, I received her phone call also. She told me that her parents may soon meet my parents to settle all issues for solemnising our marriage.

After 15 days, her parents went to my house and fixed our engagement after two months. And our marriage was scheduled two months after the engagement. We got sufficient time to firm up our mutual understanding about different marital issues. We started seeing each other quite frequently. Sometime, she used to visit Mumbai, or I used to fly to Delhi. As our proximity increased, so our strength and weaknesses also got exposed to each other. My fear of future trouble was increasing with the passage of every date, I'd with Zoya. One day, I again expressed my lingering doubt to Zoya. 'I don't think we can pull on well. It's not too late, let's call off our engagement. We may even spoil our friendship.'

'What nonsense are you talking about? I can't even think of anyone else as my husband. You're really hurting me. Never talk such rubbish in the future,' she said and hugged me. I was speechless. After a few minutes, she said, 'Let's pen down what you expect from me and what I expect from you. This may help us to control our whims and fancy. And help us making mid route corrections.'

Knowing her nature, I thought she was kidding, so I asked her, 'Are you sure you want to have a record of each other's expectations and goals of life?'

'Of course,' she said and to my utter surprise, she took out a pen and paper from her bag to write down. Seeing this, I asked her, 'If you want to maintain a record of our expectations from each other, please also note down our aspiration and goals of life. I've seen people complaining- "had they not got married, they could've done wonders in life."

Interrupting me she said, 'Very good idea.'

She actually made a statement of our goals and what we expected from each of us. She got it signed from me. I must confess, I thought it was her prank to divert my attention from the main issue. However, she kept it and that recorded statement helped us many times to solve our differences amicably and prevented a major conflict. And now, I think every couple must make a note of their goals, aspirations in life and expectations from each other before committing to marriage. However, they should ensure that their expectations are reasonable and achievable. If they find that their goals or expectations aren't matching, it's better, they should remain friends rather than getting married.

'I think, it makes sense. Had I exchanged my views with Teena about my desire to settle outside the country, she wouldn't have married me. I could've saved myself from the trauma of two years of suffering, which I experienced with her. You please continue with your story,' Raj said, while taking a big breath.

Time was fleeting and we both got lost in our marriage preparation. We got married, following all rituals and customs like that of any other arranged marriage. No doubt, I got married to Zoya with high expectations; but back of my mind, there was a lurking doubt about the possible future troubles in our relationship. Despite my intuitive feelings about future problems on account of Zoya's obstinate reactions to some issues, I couldn't muster enough courage to annul our marriage plan. All the time, my sixth sense kept on cautioning me against marriage with Zoya. It was portending me about the future turmoil to be unfolded in due course of marital life. However, I always convinced myself to have a positive attitude in life.

'Did you've any conflict with Zoya after the marriage on the counts you're fearing?' Raj asked interrupting his silence.

'As expected, we quarrelled just two days after the marriage. She was asked to cook some sweets as per our custom. She cooked Khir (sweet rice), but it wasn't fully cooked and she served it. No one liked it, except my father who complemented her for making efforts to cook. However, she felt offended when someone commented that Bhabhi Ji had put less sugar in the Khir to protect us from diabetes. She complained, 'What do you people think of me? Am I a chef, whom you've brought home to cook delicious food? I took so much pain to make khir and instead of appreciating me, you people are making fun of me.'

'What're you saying? Nobody expects you to cook regularly. I told you that you would be expected to follow some customary practices. This has been just a ritual. You're feeling bad because you're conscious of your inability to cook. So, don't try to cover up your failure by making such silly allegation. I've already warned you against all such things,' I said politely.

Instead of realising her mistake, she felt offended and countered me, 'You're blaming me. I tried my best to appease all of you. If khir wasn't fully cooked or less sweet, so what. You people should've appreciated my efforts, instead of blaming me. I mayn't cook anything in future.'

'Madam, mind your language. No one is reprimanding you. It's you, who blame herself,' I said. 'You make a mountain out of mole hill. Your attitude is louder than your words. You look for an opportunity to get rid of your domestic responsibilities. If you adopt this attitude from the beginning, I don't think you can make space for yourself in my family.'

'I'm least interested in your family's admiration,' she shot back.

'Listen, it isn't a question of your liking or disliking. It's the issue of my prestige. I don't want you to give someone a chance to criticise you. I hate people making fun of you due to your inability to handle domestic affairs.' I cautioned her and moved on.

We didn't sort it out, but tried to bury, hoping it mightn't bother us again. You know, suppressed things are bound to erupt like a volcano. We stayed with parents for a few days and then went on a honeymoon trip to Hong Kong and Singapore for two weeks. Hardly a day passed and we again had heated talk. Actually, I got my stomach upset due to very spicy food that I'd eaten for dinner. Next day, I requested her, 'I felt very sick due to eating junk food yesterday. Why don't you attempt to cook simple dal and rice for me, our apartment has a fully loaded kitchen.'

She agreed and cooked rice and lentils. However, it was so horrible, I couldn't eat it. And instead of feeling better, I was worse off.

'I think you haven't excused me for our last spat and so took advantage of my sickness to revenge your hurt feelings,' I taunted her.

'What do you mean by taking revenge? How can you think so mean to me? I can't even dream of harming you,' she said making a long face.

'It's quite obvious. You cooked such horrible food, I could hardly take a bite. I think opting for junk food would've been the better option, rather than desiring you to cook. If this type of food is served regularly, I'm afraid, I may even stop eating home food altogether.' I hardly finished my sentence, she jumped from her chair and started shouting. 'You hardly miss any opportunity to insult me. You know very well that I haven't learnt cookery, even then I tried to cook for you. Instead of appreciating my love and endeavour, you're rejoicing in criticising me. I can't cook food as your mother or sister can. So, stop comparing my food with them,' she said all this at the best of her sound pitch.

We weren't comfortable with each other at least for two days after that incident. I cursed myself as to why did I agree to marry her, knowing her stupidity and abhorrence for cooking? Actually, she thought, she can learn cooking and it shouldn't be a serious issue. But, she forgot to realise that she'd an innate disliking for cooking and she can never learn it.

We came back home after two weeks and wanted to go back to Mumbai after spending a few days in home. But, my parents insisted that Zoya should stay with them for some more time. I didn't agree and explained them that both of us had to go back to our respective work place. Somehow, they agreed reluctantly. After three days, I went to Mumbai and Zoya was back to Delhi.

On reaching Mumbai, I requested my department to post me in Delhi. My controlling officer, empathising with me, soon posted me in Delhi. In a month's time, I joined Zoya who wanted to complete her post-graduation in Delhi. She got busy with her studies and hardly had time for household activities. We engaged a regular servant to cook and look after other mundane domestic affairs. But, we used to have a real tough time, whenever servant went on leave. His absence was bound to lead us in some disastrous situation. One day, I invited my friend and his family for dinner. And servant had to suddenly go on leave to attend some emergency back home. She'd no choice but to manage herself. I came from the office and enquired about her preparedness for dinner. I was shocked to taste the food. It was unusually very tasty.

'It tastes very delicious,' I said to praise her for cooking very delicious food. 'I'm amazed to know that you've learnt cooking so fast without letting me know. Today you've prepared very delicious food. All cousins appear to be typical Rajasthan delicacies.'

'Are you kidding or really happy?' She curiously enquired while embracing me.

'Yes, I am really very happy my darling,' I said. 'I'm on top of the world to taste such mouth- watering food. I'm sure, your guest would be equally pleased to have such delicacies.'

'Your happiness has just cost me a few hundred bucks. I never realised, it's so easy to please you…'

'What do you mean- it's so easy to please you?' Interrupting her, I expressed my surprise.

'You should know, I haven't cooked this food, but I ordered it from a restaurant. It means you also love market food, which's certainly tastier than home food,' she informed me very joyfully.

'I appreciate your management skill. But, it's disgusting to compare home cooked food with that of a restaurant. You don't realise that no one can eat every day in a hotel or restaurant. Besides being costly, it isn't conducive for a healthy life to dine out every day,' I said to express my reservation.

'Honey! You're unnecessarily flaring it up. Let's enjoy this evening and forget who cooked the food,' she said very lovingly.

'No, dear, it's you, who's trivialising one of the major concerns any family can have,' I said a bit rudely.

It sparked a big debate and almost spoiled that evening. In retrospect, I realised that I had unnecessarily dragged the issue. I should've appreciated her tactfulness to manage the dinner, which really pleased the guests.

Next day, I talked to her and expressed my apology. 'My darling, I'm extremely sorry for what happened yesterday,' I said. 'You really managed the evening very well in the absence of the servant. It was I, who couldn't appreciate your efforts and blamed you for fetching food from the market. Had you cooked yourself, perhaps, guest mightn't have enjoyed the dinner, as they actually did yesterday. Everything went very well. Hence forth, I shouldn't have any objection for outsourcing food to host dinner. It may be equally good if you can hire a caterer for that evening.'

She smiled and said, 'I've already forgotten, what you said yesterday. You know, I don't normally feel bad, what you say. I know, you really love me and have no intention to hurt me.'

'You're really great. I'm lucky to have you as my wife. I love you,' I said and kissed her. Since then, I hardly made food an issue to obviate any dispute on this count.

'Did you've some other differences or just food was the only a big cause of conflict?' Breaking his silence, Raj enquired.

Certainly there're many other issues and one of them was our different time schedule. I'd regular office hours, except when I had to go out in odd hours to attend some emergent situations or meetings. Besides, sometimes, I'd to go on official tours. However, Zoya had no fixed timings, her duties used to change fortnightly. Quite often, she used to get held up till midnight to attend medical emergencies. On many occasions, our evening got spoiled due to her emergent professional calls. This started creating some fissures in our family relations. Many times, it resulted in heated discussions and altercations, particularly when some friends or relatives were invited by her and she failed to show up. This used to create a very embarrassing situation for me. Things used to get flared up whenever she visited her relatives after her work without informing me. In those days mobile phones weren't available and land line phones used to be out of order quite often. Once our fight was so severe that we almost decided to quit our relationship. When temper subsided, we both realised our follies and felt sorry to each other.

Time was passing and Zoya was neither improving her lifestyle, nor conduct. Her peevish behaviour was making our relations unbearable. And one day, I decided to take the bull by horn to find a way of preventing day to day bickering. It was a beautiful Sunday morning and we both had a holiday. I was reading newspaper while relaxing in a rocking chair. She was also in a good mood. She brought tea for me and while putting the tray on the table, she said, 'Enjoy your tea.'

When she was about to move, I held her hand and said, 'I would like to enjoy my tea in your company. I hope you won't mind it.'

'How romantic? Why should I mind it? I always look for such occasions, when you're so happy and romantic,' she said and sat down on a chair lying in front of me. She made tea and offered it with a query, 'What's your plan for the day? Are you taking me out for lunch?'

'Why not? Today, we can go out for lunch. It's long due. Where do you like to book your table my darling?' I enquired.

'Wherever you take me, I'll go with your choice,' she said to leave it to my decision.

'Zoya. I've something more serious to talk to you than lunch venue,' I said to look for an opportunity to thrash out our conflicts.

'What's so serious that you want to deliberate with me so early in the morning?' She questioned, while showing her surprise.

'You know life is too short to make love and we keep on wasting our precious time in fighting with each other. Why don't we settle our fissures, which bitters our relations?' I said.

'Don't spoil my mood by raising old issues,' she said, while expressing her unwillingness to have any serious discussion about our differences.

'I think we must sort out our differences,' I said.

'I don't want to dwell over them to make your tea taste bitter,' she replied.

'I may also not like to spoil such a beautiful day,' I said. 'You know whole week, both of us remain so busy that we hardly get time to chat with each other. It's necessary, we must spend some time together to understand each other's perspective to sort out the issues, which destroy our peace and harmonious relation. I'm sure, you would love to see me smiling most of the time and chatting with you.'

'Who may like to see her husband's long face or him in a pugnacious mood all the time? At least, I would be the last one. Please tell me, what's in your mind?' She said grumblingly.

'You know, I'm a slave to my taste buds and hence don't expect you or anyone else serving me bad food, which makes me lose all my senses. It's a fact that you can't cook good food, let's accept this. Perhaps, this was one of the reasons of my reluctance to marry…'

'You mean to say, you wanted to leave me just because I don't know how to cook. How mean are you?' Interrupting me, she cried.

'Do I say so? Please listen and don't interrupt me,' I said very politely. 'Having realised that cooking isn't your cup of tea, I've decided to get our servant trained in cooking, since we can afford it. This'll solve our problem. I may get food of my choice and you won't be bothered to cook. You'll have time to chat with me. Whenever the servant goes on leave, we may take off to visit our parents and don't invite anyone in his absence.'

She kept silence for a few seconds and then got up. She came to my back and rested both of her elbows on my respective shoulders. Then she held my chin with her right hand's palm and pressed it upwards very gently to lift my face. She looked in my eyes for a moment, then bended and kissed my forehead, while saying, 'I love you. Do you really love me?'

'Of course, I love you. I thought life is too short to fight on such trivial matters. So, I thought of this. If you aren't in the kitchen, I may get more of your company and attention. Secondly, your time is more precious and it should be used either for me or for patients to save their life,' I said smiling and caressing her hand.

'Oh, how sweet of you. You're right, I don't have time for cooking, even though I can learn it. I'll get more time to spend with you. I'm thankful to God for blessing me with such an affectionate and loving husband,' she said fondling my hair.

'Are you really happy?' I asked and without waiting for her reply, I further said, 'I don't know about you, but I'm sure about myself. I'll be saved from the ordeal of having your food.'

'Hey, are you making fun of me?' She said and started hammering my chest as if she was really furious and showing her anger, but careful not to hurt me. I held her hands and said, 'You've made my day.' And pulled her on my lap.

She cooled down and said, 'I know you'll not miss any chance to tease me.'

'I believe after that you didn't have any fight on account of unpleasant meal?' Raj commented, interrupting me impatiently.

'Do you think life is so simple? It was hardly two weeks thereafter, we're again on cross firing. One day, I came from the office and found she was in home. To my utter surprise, she was in the kitchen and busy in cooking something. 'It's strange to find you in the kitchen,' I said loudly, while laughing. 'May I know, who's going to be your prey, my sweet heart?'

'Of course you, who can be better than you? Can you ever talk nicely to me? I'm making pudding and cake for you as per the new recipe, I have learnt from my friend,' she replied, while suppressing her anger and giving a smiling look.

'Honey, I'm honoured and will be privileged to taste it. May I take a quick shower and get ready to celebrate this occasion,' I said and left her in the kitchen to take a quick shower.

When I came back to the living room, I saw she'd laid the table and was waiting for me to join. I joined her and took a piece of pudding, she'd made for me. I tasted it. Pudding was really very tasty.

'Oh! I wasn't expecting it to taste so delicious,' I said and kissed her.

'Thanks. Now taste this cake,' she requested, while offering a piece of cake.

I took that piece of cake from her hand and tasted it. I spat as I chewed it and cried, 'What the hell you've made. It's bitterly salty.'

She was totally lost and looked bewildered and perplexed. She also quickly tasted the same cake and rushed back to the kitchen. After a few minutes, she cried, 'Accidently, I've mixed the salt in place of sugar. I'm very sorry.'

Instead of appreciating her efforts to cook something good for me, I scolded her. 'When you don't know how to cook, why do you meddle with cooking business?'

Hearing this, she got furious and lost her temper. 'Are you really the same Jai I knew- a very compassionate and caring one? I took so much pain for you to learn cooking, so that I can please you. And, just for a small and unintended mistake, you're slighting me. Hence forth, I'll never enter in the kitchen, I promise.' She said and left the dining hall.

'I think your reaction was unpalatable and uncalled for. You should've appreciated her spirit, instead of finding a fault,' said Raj.

'You're absolutely on the mark. This happens with most of us,' I said. 'We take our spouse for granted about everything. We think it's her sacrosanct duty to cook every day tasty food for her family, without making any mistake. We forget that women are also human beings. They're as fallible as men, being a creation of the same God, who created men. After a while, I also realised my mistake and went to Zoya to express my apology; but she was unrelenting and didn't speak to me. In a few days, however, she was normal.'

'Had you not been able to afford a full time cook, what steps would've you taken to address such a situation?' Asked Raj.

'Everything has a price. If food is so dear to me, I'll have no option, but to learn cooking myself. I don't see any logic, which makes us believe that cooking is the sole domain of a housewife. If both of us are working, whether wife knows cooking or not, both of us need to share the pain and pleasure together. Both should cooperate with each other in doing work together- be it cooking, dishwashing, household purchasing, entertaining of guests or helping children to do their homework etc. We simply can't get away from all these responsibilities by saying all these're the concern of a wife. If we ignore these hard realities, our life boat is bound to navigate through choppy water and we won't know when it sinks in deep water to never surface again.' I explained to Raj my vantage point.

'I highly appreciate your outlook towards married life. Hope, you didn't have any fissure after that.' Raj further enquired.

'Since that incident, I tried to restrain my impulsive and critical behaviour. She was also careful. You know, there're many issues in married life, which always keep you on tenterhook. One of them is jealousness. Your wife or girlfriend can never tolerate your good words about other women or her friends. One Sunday, I was reading a newspaper, when Zoya came to serve me tea. Suddenly, the doorbell started ringing.

I tried to get up to check the visitor. She pushed me down on the chair and said, 'My dear, you enjoy your newspaper. I'm going to see who's come so early in the morning to disturb our privacy.'

In a few minutes, she started calling me, 'Jai come here. See! Who has come?

I rushed to the door. I saw, some beautiful lady was hugging Zoya.

Seeing me, Zoya said, 'Meet my dear friend-Seri Pandia.'

'Hi, I'm Jai. You're welcome to our house,' I said to greet her friend.

She smiled and shook hands with me, while lifting her bag from her left hand. She was a very pretty and smart lady in her early thirties. Zoya requested her to get in the house. Seri moved forward and Zoya followed her. I held the Zoya's hand to whisper in her ear, 'Where was she hiding herself all these years? Why didn't I see her with you before or after our marriage, if she's your rattling dear friend?'

'Behave yourself. What'll she think of you- a beast, who's never lived in a civilised society and seen a beautiful girl?' She said, while pushing me away from herself. She made Seri seated comfortably on the couch, lying in the drawing room. She asked her, 'Did you've any problem in locating our house?'

'Absolutely not. I'd your address and the driver was knowing this area, so he brought me straight to your house, without any difficulty,' said Seri very affectionately.

'It's nice to meet you, after a long time,' said Zoya.

Seri had perhaps heard my remark, hence addressing us she said, 'Zoya you know, I'd been in the USA from last two years in regard to my study, so I didn't meet you and even couldn't attend your wedding. I wanted to surprise you, hence didn't inform you about my visit. I checked from your office, which informed me that you are in the city and attending hospital regularly. Having being confident that you're at home, I came to your house. Hope, you people don't feel offended by my uninformed arrival.'

'Not at all. You did the right thing. You're more than welcome to visit our house. It'll be our pleasure to host you,' I said, suppressing my unwarranted enthusiasm.

Zoya asked our servant-Subhash to serve tea and snacks to Seri. I unwillingly excused myself to give both the friends some privacy to catch up with each other. She spent about two hours with Zoya and thereafter left for Mumbai. When Zoya was back after seeing her off, I said, 'Your friend appears very interesting. You should've requested her to stay for lunch.'

'I see, you're showing more interest in her than required. She's to visit her parents. She may join my hospital in a couple of weeks and may come someday to spend time with us,' Zoya informed me and left the drawing room.

After some time, Seri joined Zoya's hospital and started visiting our house quite frequently. Over a period of time, I became quite friendly with her. Occasionally, her husband also used to come along with her. He was also an interesting guy. Later on, I came to know that they weren't on good terms, despite the fact that Seri's husband was one of her distant relatives. I wondered, why she wasn't having a happy married life, particularly, when she got married in her own community and that too with her relative. She'd an arranged marriage and not a love marriage. They should've been a very happily married couple.

'This proves marriage within the community is no guarantee for a happy married life,' Jai commented. 'Sorry for interrupting you. Please continue with your story.'

Seri used to bring something for me whenever she visited my house. It was one of the Sundays, when she came to see us. I'd some tiff with Zoya on the previous night and was non-communicative with her. I was reading a newspaper sitting alone in my balcony, adjacent to my bedroom, when she came to our house. She saw me sitting alone. She guessed my mood and sat down beside me.

'It appears that you didn't have peaceful sleep last night. Perhaps, your dream girl had been haunting you throughout the night. Be cheerful like this flower,' she said, while presenting to me a red rose with a big smile on her face. I was really thrilled and happily accepted her flower. I called my servant and asked him to serve tea and snacks to her. My wife was watching all this, but said nothing at that time. I don't know what transpired between them and Seri never came to our house since that day. I enquired about her from Zoya numerous time, but she'd been always elusive.

One day, when I pestered Zoya to know about Seri, she exploded, 'How could I tolerate a lady presenting a red rose to my husband and that too in my presence? Seri had exceeded her limits, so she'd to go from your life. I've allowed her to see me alone. She's still in touch with me.'

'How can you be so mean? She's an excellent person and your best friend. How can you treat her like this? What she'll think about me-just a philanderer. It's shame on you to distrust me.' I scolded Zoya for her uncalled for behaviour.

This's one of the incidents which strained our relation for a while. Time is a great healer and with the passage of time I forgot her. I must confess, barring that incident, there hadn't been any other occasion when Zoya ever suspected me. She never enquired from me, where do I go, whom do I meet with, or why do I come so late? I've been lucky in a sense that I've never been put to the litmus test of fidelity, which perhaps hardly any married person can elude.

'What's your secret? I'd faced this ordeal very often from my both the wives. Sometimes, I had to stay quite late in the office, or occasionally got home late because of official parties. And, I was bound to be questioned on home. I didn't know how to save myself from their gruelling and investigative questions. Their sarcasms and queries had been too tortuous to frighten me enter my own house,' said Raj to share his miseries.

'Zoya has magnanimity to maintain her composure. Most of the time, she won't raise her voice or show her anger, even if I reach home quite late at night. On the contrary, I may be very unhappy and even shout, if she gets late. Similarly, unlike other women, she's never demanded any gift or presents from me on any occasion. I can only say, I'm lucky or she's exceptionally generous,' I said.

'It means no acrimony spoiled your marital bliss on these counts, unlike me who suffered miserably due to mutual distrust?' Raj enquired hiding his curiousness.

'You know, human relations are very complex. We'd our share of acrimonious relations, but certainly not on distrust count.

Zoya loves shopping. She'd been a profligate spender for a long time after marriage. She splurged all her salary on shopping. I didn't say much till she was working and earning enough to pay bills for all her purchases. After the birth of our son, she quit her job and opened her own clinic. Once she started her clinic, her earning wasn't stable, but she didn't change her spending habits. She used to buy lots of toys, dresses and other gifts for me, her son, friends and relatives. She may even spend in anticipation of her earnings. She always had some outstanding bills, which occasionally used to trigger the volcano to devastate our peace. Her only defence was I don't waste money and I can account for it. One day, some old friends were to come for dinner and she asked for money, 'Dear, can you give me some money to buy grocery.'

'I've given you enough money to buy monthly groceries. How come it's over in a fortnight?' I said.

'I'm sorry to tell you that this month I haven't bought monthly grocery. I've some old bills to clear, so I used the money you gave to square them up. I may repay you, once I get my money. Today, please give me some amount to buy grocery.' She said all this very coolly.

I got very angry and shouted, 'You think, I've a money plant and can give you any amount, whenever you so desire. I can't give you any money,' I said to express my anguish.

'If you don't give me money, I won't be able to entertain your friends and then don't blame me,' she said and got up to leave the drawing room.

'You're blackmailing me for ransom. You know, I can't afford if my friends are ill-treated. Would you have behaved in the same fashion, had I invited your relatives? I'm sure, in that case, you would've managed yourself without telling me anything,' I said.

'Dear, don't make it an issue. I'm serious, I don't have any money. Your friends are coming, so I'm asking for money. The situation won't have been different in case my friends or relatives were to come. I would've still requested you to give me money,' she said, while explaining her situation.

'I can give you money, but tell me how long you want to pull on like this. You spend not only your entire earning, but also hardly save anything from my salary. We don't lead life better than those whose wives aren't working. As a housewife, they give full attention to their family and, at least, their children aren't fed and nourished by their made servants. What're you doing? Neither can you look after your home, nor your profession.' I expressed my grudge against her.

'You want me to remain in home and spend my rest of life in the kitchen to feed you and your children. You know, I won't do it. I'm working so that I can support myself and not dependent on any one for my personal needs,' she said, while seriously protesting to my comment.

'Great, you're working to support yourself. Then why're you asking for money? Don't you think, it's insulting for you?' I retorted.

'Don't give me money. I may manage it and henceforth I'll never ask for money from you,' she said, expressing her frustration.

I left for my office. Such incidents were common and used to spoil our relations quite often. That day, before going to the office, I phoned to the shopkeeper, who used to regularly supply us grocery, to give grocery to my servant as per the list.

I gave some money to my servant and advised him to get the grocery from that shop. Thus, situation was managed.

Since that incident, I decided to do all monthly purchasing myself to avoid this type of bickering in the future. This gave me a lot of peace.

'You mean, you'd been managing domestic business all these years,' said Raj to express his anxiety and surprise.

'Not at all. It was hardly a few months, when I ran the show. Initially she thought, I won't be able to run the house. She observed, I wasn't complaining about anything and attending all household matters, despite my busy official schedule. She apologised and took over the domestic responsibilities. As I told you, Zoya is very considerate and can't see me suffering. She transformed herself and changed her spending habits. She became very judicious in expenditure and started discussing with me before making any big purchase. But all this took a long time to transform her. Had I behaved as per my impulsive characteristic, we would've parted long back. And everything could've been attributed to love marriage as a major cause of failure of marriage.

'No doubt, one should manage his or her financial matters wisely to live within one's own resources,' said Raj. 'Finance can certainly spoil one's relation, if one profligates beyond his capacity. But, I must say, you handled your wife very wisely like your any other official engagement.'

'You need to have patience and endurance to appreciate your wife's views and reasons for her particular reaction or conduct. To understand Zoya's profligacy, I analysed her nature and grooming. I found Zoya's parents were ready to give her any amount of money, without trying to know where and how she spends. This had incapacitated her to appreciate the value of money. Having discovered this, I made her realise that she's no more a child of her parents, but an independent married woman having her own house and family distinct from her parents. She shouldn't ask for money from her parents to maintain her self-respect. She should learn how to live within her own resources. I'd taken lessons from my previous broken relations. My short lived friendship with Mamta and Roni was a blessing in disguise for my stable marital life. I realised individual's grooming play a vital role in shaping one's personality and influencing his conduct and reactions. Zoya's profligacy was attributable to her childhood environment,' I said to share my experience and observation about Zoya.

'I agree that socio-economic and family values play a critical role in making your personality. But, I perceive another reason for differential male and female behaviour. Most of us don't realise and understand that male and female are totally different human beings. They see things differently, they feel differently and think differently from each other. Consequently, they're bound to have variance in their opinion, reaction or point of view about the same thing,' said Raj to share his views.

'I fully agree with you,' I said. 'Perhaps, that's the reason male and female have been assigned different roles to play in their family and social life. I've seen my mother devoting her full time to look after us and all other household affairs. The rearing of the children had never been a cause of concern to my father, who didn't know how to make tea, what to say about cooking one time meal. My father used to show his unhappiness about something just by rupturing his communication with my mother. His way of conducting himself, knowingly and unknowingly, shaped my behaviour and reactions. I didn't bother to know what made Mamta or Roni to act in a manner which offended me. I abruptly terminated my relationship with both of them. Quite late, I realised the difference between male and female perception towards life, you're referring to. Most of the time, people don't accept this universal fact and expect others to behave and think similar to them. This becomes a potential cause of individual belligerency and distrust in married life. This's one of the reasons, you can't have a perfect partner. It's you, who've to make your relation perfect by complementing each other. You've to see her actions from her perceptions and not from that of yours alone...'

'I appreciate your point of view. But, very often, we react in haste and refuse to accept our own mistake even after realising it. Our ego prevents us from doing so. That's why an educated person may've a disastrous married life and an uneducated one can enjoy the fruits of a happy married life, if he follows what you say,' said Raj, while interrupting me.

'Raj, it isn't an issue of being educated or uneducated. It's the issue of being sensitive to the basic difference between male and female. If you're sensitive and appreciate this difference, you can empathise with your spouse and minimise chances of conflict. You may still have some differences, despite empathising with your darling, as expectations and aspirations keep on changing with the time and situation...'

'Hold on. If someone strictly follows your advice, people may consider him week and timid. He may be called 'Joru ka Gulam' (wife's slave). And it isn't always practical to make inquisitions about the conditions, which affected the grooming of your spouse,' said Raj, while again interrupting me.

'You're right. Sometimes, you may feel cheated, because your gentleness and compassion may be treated as your weakness to yield under pressure. Quite often, you're forced to accept unreasonable or ridiculous demands of your insensitive partner. This happens and can't be denied. But, instead of trying to mend her behaviour by your disapprovals or criticism alone, you need to agonise for making your partner realise the consequences of her conducts and appreciate your perception of life. And for that, you may be required to look into her past,' I said.

'Do you think, patience and endurance can solve most of the marital differences, if married couple accept the basic difference between male and female's perception?' Raj sought an explanation.

'I think so. No doubt, differences may continue to exist till you're alive, as you don't live in static conditions. All living beings keep on evolving and changing their needs as per requirement of the time. Hence, they can't be given similar treatment all the time. I simply say, conflicts cannot be eliminated from your life. However, patience and endurance can help you to minimise them in order to maintain better cordial relations in a married life,' I said to further explain my view.

'So, you accept that conflict can't be eliminated in married life, but these can be minimised. Have your darling ever fought with you on account of issues like your life style or in-laws etc.? Raj further enquired.

'Zoya wasn't eating many vegetables, which I and my family used to eat. It necessitated cooking of three to four types of dishes every day to satiate differential taste buds of each member of the family. This used to strain family relations, whenever she visited my home or my parents came to our place. Similarly, she can't tolerate hunger; hence she never observed fasting on any occasion, be it 'Karvachauth or any other festival requiring fasting,' I said. 'You know, Karwachauth is a fasting festival or ritual observed annually by most of the Hindu married women to pray for the longevity of their husbands. Initially, my mother didn't like her to avoid fasting, however, it didn't gravitate into a big issue. Actually non observance of Karwchauth by Zoya is attributed to her mother, who herself never observed it. That may be one of the reasons for her reluctance to follow the tradition. We've to accept that a woman can't adopt her extended family's customs overnight and abruptly forget her own traditions and practices, with which she's grown through a period. However, most of us expect our partners to adopt all our family habits and customs in a day to behave like any other member of her extended family. This's an unreasonable expectation. But, it becomes one of the potential causes of a family dispute, if your partner is unable to adopt changed environment quickly,' I said.

'I see, you've made quite interesting observations about married life. How come you know so much about marital discords? Raj enquired.

'I've been a keen observer of family disputes from my childhood. I've seen some of my relatives and friends leading a blissful married life. While others losing their peace and pleasure due to their inability to appease their darlings, whom they married to lead a happy life. Besides, I've read lots of stories and research papers, published in newspapers and magazines, about reasons of success and failure of marriages,' I said.

'Great. No wonder, that's why, you've been giving me sermons so far…'

'I haven't given you any sermons so far. I've either made my observation or shared my experience with you. I know, it's easy to preach rather than to practice,' I said, while interrupting him.

'Don't feel offended. Just jesting. I've no intention to slight you. I actually appreciate your endurance to keep your darling happy. Now, you tell me how did you manage your parents and in-laws? Did you ever have any dispute with Zoya on this count?' Raj enquired, while defending himself.

'I don't think, we'd any big dispute on account of our parents. Once my parents came to our house after marriage, and my mother started directing my servants how to manage a home and what to cook. I saw Zoya, getting upset and confused. I told my mother, 'Mom, you're very nice. You still take so much pain to look after me. You want to feed me the same way as you used to do in my childhood. However, now I expect you to take a rest and don't do anything till you're with me. I'll be very happy to see you relaxing and treating your stay with us as a holiday. You may tell Zoya or servant to cook whatever you want to eat. You live the way you want to live, but please don't direct us how to live or how to manage our affairs.' My mother became very unhappy, listening my request. She started rebuking me. But, she cooled down as my father said, 'Jai has really grown up and I'm happy to know he can manage his family affairs very well. Please don't say anything to him.' It was enough to silence my mother. She didn't say anything further...'

'How come you could say all this to your mother? Most of us can't dare?' Interrupting me, Raj said.

'You know Raj. Every marriage entails leaving of old bonding with parents and siblings to give way for new ties and bonding with your spouse and her family. It means, you must leave your parents to become one flesh to unite and bond with your spouse. You get a new life and existence. However, this doesn't mean you show disrespect to your parents or jettison them or disown your responsibilities towards them. It means, you won't be banking on them for their guidance and help for all your day to day activities. Instead, you'll give much credence to your spouse and share your feelings first with your darling and then with others. This helps your spouse feel respected and loved...'

'I value your observation. Now, I see that I didn't make efforts to bond with my wife. I'd been taking most of the decision on my own, without involving her,' said Raj, while again interrupting me. 'Please continue your story.'

'Similarly, parents are required to refrain from giving unsolicited advice, money, or criticize decisions and conducts of their children. They've to give a chance to their children to err and learn themselves. What I said to my mother was needed to keep me off from her lap. After that day, my mother never interfered in my family affairs. Interference, in the children's family affairs by their parents, is one of the major causes of divorce as per my lawyer friend,' I said.

'What you say is really true. I know a number of cases where divorce took place because of the parents' interference. Actually, parents remain sceptical about the welfare of their children, particularly about their daughters. They start enquiring, from the very next day of marriage, about the treatment being given to their daughters by different members of the husband's family. They start suggesting and guiding their daughters without knowing full context and backgrounds. And if a girl starts acting as per the advice of their parents or relatives, she's bound to make her life hell. She shouldn't approach her parents, until she's actually given bad treatment by their in laws. Jai, it's good to know that you didn't have any problem from your in laws.' Raj commented.

'You shouldn't conclude that I didn't have any problem from my in-laws. There had been some conflict between my mother and my mother-in-law about the treatment required for nurturing of my son. When my wife was expecting, her mother came a few days before her delivery. My mother came a few days after my son's birth. Her mother used to massage my son with butter oil and my mother wanted my son to be massaged with mustard oil, being antiseptic. Similarly, her mother wanted Zoya to eat lots of dry fruits and fried stuffs to gain strength. Whereas, my mother wanted Zoya to avoid fried and heavy stuffs so that she shouldn't put on weight. Both were well-wishers of Zoya, but had a different approach as per their grooming. They couldn't pull on for more than a week and both of our well-wishers went back to their respective places, leaving Zoya alone to take care of herself and her son. This really flustered us and we got worried about our son. But, somehow, we managed with the help of a maid…'

Interrupting me Raj commented, 'I also faced almost a similar situation when my mother in law visited our house at the time of birth of my daughter. My aunt and Teena's mother used to quarrel each day on some pretext. Such relatives are a big pain to young couples. They need to be handled with care. Since my father was an old friend of Teena's father, he could manage the situation. Please continue your story.'

'There'd been no difference between mine and her father. Both got well with each other. Similarly, my sisters befriended Zoya quickly. There'd been hardly any differences between them. It was my younger brother's wife who didn't like Zoya, but she seldom exhibited her dislike to Zoya in her conducts. On the contrary, it was her aunt, a younger sister of Zoya's mother, who became a real Villon in our relation. Zoya was reared by her maternal grandmother. So, she spent a good part of her life with her aunt, who's about ten years elder to Zoya. Thus, she'd a deep rooted fascination for her aunt, whom she used to bank on for all her emotional issues. Apparently, her aunt was a very sweet and cordial lady, but a very selfish and immature person. Money is her God. She thinks money can buy anything and everything. She used to bring lots of gifts and presents whenever she visits our house. However, I never considered her a sensible person. I may give you just one example to assess her true nature. One day, she came rushing to our house and wanted Zoya to accompany her to Rangoon for handling any urgent business issue of her company. That time my son was just four months old.

'I got a very urgent matter in Rangoon and need your help to sort it out,' her aunt said. 'Your uncle can't go there due to his other pre-engagements. He's asked me to visit Rangoon along with Zoya. I'll be really obliged, if you permit Zoya to accompany me. We'll be back in just two days.'

'What're you saying? Who'll feed my son Nik, who's living on his mother's feed? Do you think Zoya can afford to go out, leaving her four months old son back home? I'm afraid to say, I can't help you,' I said disapproving her request.

'Jai, it's a matter of just two days only. I know you can manage Nik. Maid can feed him with bottled milk. It shouldn't be very difficult to manage just for two days.' She pleaded to persuade me.

'What do you think Zoya?' I asked my wife, who was standing close to me, hearing our conversation quietly so far.

'Jai, aunty is really in a serious mess, that's why she's seeking our help. I can help her provided you agree,' she said.

'What! Are you mad? How can you accompany aunt leaving your son to the mercy of a maid? Are you sure, you can afford loss of two day's breast feeding to Nik?' I questioned Zoya, while staring her in disgust, on knowing her willingness to visit Rangoon particularly when Nik was on her feed.

'She may've irreparable loss, if she doesn't go to Rangoon to attend her business. Whereas, loss of two day's breast feeding can be compensated. If you agree to cooperate, I may like to help her out,' she said to emphasize her willingness to accompany her aunt.

'Okay. If you're so generous and keen to help her out, leaving your infant son to the mercy of a maid, how can I've any objection?' I said rudely and reluctantly.

Zoya left for Rangoon in the next four days. I took leave to take care of my son. She came back after four days instead of two days. Since those days mobile phone services weren't available, I couldn't communicate with her to know the reasons of her delay. When she came back after four days, it was revealed to me that her aunt didn't go along with my wife. It was Zoya, who alone managed her business affairs. This incident peeved me so much so that we didn't have normal relations for a quite some time. I was unhappy with my wife and her aunt, who didn't dare to enter my house for a long time. However, she joined us for the occasion of my son's birthday and after that she again started visiting us regularly. Whenever Zoya visited her place or her aunt came to our place, we'd some unpleasant happenings. One day our differences reached a flash point to call the attention of my father- in- law. He intervened and warned Zoya to avoid the company of her aunt. We spent some time happily without her intervention. However, hardly a few months might've passed when she again visited to my house on the occasion of Diwali festival with lots of sweets and fruits.

'Hi, Jai, how're you?' was her routine greeting with a big smile on her face.

I was really shocked to see her, but, hiding my anger and hate, I responded, 'I'm fine, hope uncle and everyone must be fine in your home.'

'Oh yes, we're really thankful to you for helping us out in solving our problem. Your uncle was remembering you. He was very keen to meet you. However, he couldn't manage to come along with me due to some urgent work. He asked me to give you these sweets to thank for all your cooperation and help extended to us,' she said with her usual smile, while presenting a sweets box to me.

'It's fine. I think, it's your niece who really helped you. It'll be nice, if you present this sweets box to her,' I said, while refusing to accept her sweets box.

'It's a fact that Zoya was really a great help to us. However, she couldn't have gone to Rangoon to help us, had you not consented and agreed to take care of your little master,' she said very affectionately.

'I would've never agreed, had I known that you're planning to send Zoya alone. How can you do that? I'm sure, you wouldn't have sent your own daughter, if she'd a small kid to feed,' I said disapproving her conduct.

'I'm really very sorry for that. I was scheduled to go along with Zoya, but for last minute glitches in visa, I couldn't go with her. It'll never happen again,' she said apologetically.

'It's all right. Let's close that topic. I hope you'll not interfere in our matter in future,' I said and left the room.

Hardly a month passed, her aunt invited us for dinner. I couldn't go due to my pre-engagement, but Zoya went. When I reached home, I found Zoya wasn't back home. I telephoned Zoya, who informed me that her aunt had requested her to stay for the night and she had agreed. I didn't say much and put the phone receiver down. Next day, I left the house early morning for my official tour, without waiting for Zoya to come back. When I came back the other day, I found Zoya was still in her aunt's house. I phoned her to know she stayed back, as I was away on tour. Next day, she came back with lots of gifts. I didn't like and condemned her for accepting gifts.

'You can't hold your greed. You're sold out to all these gifts. It was your lust for outing, and not compassion for your aunt, which prompted you to visit Rangoon leaving your four months old son to his own fate,' I scolded her.

'It's absolutely wrong. You wrongly allege me. I just wanted to help her. How can I refuse her, if she offers me some gifts? I can't be rude to displease her just like that,' Zoya protested.

'You can't displease your aunt, but you can certainly do it to me. You love to protect your aunt's interest at the cost your son…'

'Don't try to humiliate me on the pretext of my son,' said Zoya, while interrupting me.

'If you're so proud of your aunt better you go and stay with her. She can look after you better than me,' I said and left the room. Such situation occurs, when your spouse isn't able to come out of her old bonding to unite with you as one flesh. The continuance of bonding and affiliation of any spouse with her parents or relatives hampers growth of cordial relations between husband and wife. Zoya wasn't realising that her affection to her aunt was really taking its toll on our relation. She was neglecting her family responsibilities. Thus, our relations started deteriorating with every passing day and we started avoiding each other. Instead of restoring each other's emotional confidence, we indulged in sarcasm and hurled all types of attributes- stupid, cheater, mean, why I married, etc. We didn't realise that prolonging any conflict, beyond a point, was bound to close our hearts and making us less sensitive to each other's emotions…'

Interrupting me, Raj enquired, 'You mean to say, you weren't in talking terms with Zoya. How could you resolve your differences without discussing with her?

'You're right. No conflict can get resolved without discussion and in a trust deficit environment or with a bellicose mood. You need to discuss your problem in an amicable and friendly ambience. If you use abusive words or phrases, be sure to flare up the conflict leading to termination of the relation. Once you abuse your partner, retaliation is bound to take place. Similarly, Zoya became more aggressive in blame game to defend herself. As the blame game increased, it hardened our attitude and differences, instead of getting narrowed, it actually widened'

'You're sounding wise, but what happened to you? Again interrupting me Raj enquired, without suppressing his anxiousness.

'We became victims of the blame game and reached to the brink of break off. One day, I came from the office and found that Zoya wasn't at home. I enquired from Subhash, who informed me that her mother and aunt had come. And all of them had gone to market along with my son. I waited for them to come back. It was almost dinner time, when I got a phone call from Zoya.

'Jai, I'm sorry, I couldn't tell you that today is my aunt's birthday. Mummy has come and she wants you to come and join her birthday party,' she said to inform me.

'How can you behave so irresponsibly? Subhash has already cooked dinner. You must be aware about the party. So you should've instructed him accordingly. The wastage of food could've been avoided. You enjoy the party, I'm not going to come. I'll be very happy, if you stay there and don't come back. I was a pudding head to marry you,' I said and put the receiver down.

She again phoned and tried to persuade me. She apologetically said, 'I'm really very sorry for this mistake. Please don't make it an issue. You come here and I assure you, I'll come back along with you. I've no intention to stay here.'

I didn't respond and disconnected the phone. Next day, she came back and we'd a good fight.

Raising the issue, Zoya said, 'You didn't attend the party. Everyone, present there, enquired about you. It was very embarrassing for me to explain your absence. I don't know, why'd you behave so strangely? Believe me. I didn't remember her birthday and there wasn't any prior information about her birthday party; otherwise, I would've certainly informed you. You're developing a habit to make a mountain out of the molehill…'

I banged the table and interrupting her said, 'Enough is enough. I'm fed up with your concoctions and can't bear with you anymore. It was the biggest blunder of my life to marry you. I was fearing this to happen. That's why, I was reluctant to marry you. You can't realise that you've some responsibilities for your family. Whenever you feel like moving anywhere, you just leave the house. If I ask you to visit my home, you'll have ten excuses and the biggest one is your professional commitment. But the moment your aunt or any of your relative comes in the picture, your all professional commitment vanish in thin air. And you'll give the highest priority to your own family members. Let's have divorce, so that you can lead a happy, independent life,' I said all this in a fit of anger.

Retaliating me, she said, 'If you think you've really done a great sin marrying me, it's better, you atone it to get salvation.

I'll have no objection. It'll be a good riddance. I'll also get rid of the day to day bickering. I'm also fed up and can't bear it anymore.'

We both left the drawing room and went to separate bedrooms. That day, I couldn't sleep. I meditated hours to understand what was happening around me. I wondered, I'm supposed to manage thousands of people, but unable to manage my family. It's really shameful for me. When we didn't know each other, we came so close that we got married to spend the rest of our life together. And now, in just four years, we think we can't live together anymore. It can't be her fault alone. I must be having my own share too. This pricked my conscience. I got scared to face my parents. What I'll tell them that I failed to manage my affairs. I analysed my conduct over the last one year. It was an agonizing two hours brooding to realise that I was equally responsible to create an atmosphere of distrust, making Zoya emotionally very sick and insecure. I realised that a girl leaves her entire family to join her husband in a hope of leading a better life than what she'd in her parents' home. She unshackles old ties to make new relations and bonding. It isn't a small sacrifice. She can feel comfortable in a new environment, if she's loved and respected not less than what she got in her own home. The moment she feels safe and secure in her new ambience, her ties with her parents and family can take a back seat. If she still relies on her parents or relatives, it means enough emotional and financial security hasn't been given to her as per her expectation. If Zoya still gives priority to her aunt or her parents, perhaps, it's my failure to win over her confidence, which certainly can't be gained through a blame game. I saw my watch, it was showing 1.30 a.m. I went to Zoya's room and saw she was also awake. I went near to her and put my hand on her shoulder.

Squeezing her shoulder, I said, 'I'm really very sorry. I hadn't had any intention to hurt you. You know very well, I lose my temper when I don't find you at home. I've requested you many times to complete all your outdoor work before I'm back home. But, you don't heed my request. Please excuse me for all the nonsense, I said to you. I assure you not to commit such stupidity in future.'

Listening this Zoya started crying, as if she was just looking for an opportunity to vent her agony. She said, while sobbing, 'I also feel very sorry. I shouldn't have gone out without informing you. I shouldn't have spoken harsh words to you. I can't think of living without you. I'm really very sorry, please excuse me.' She couldn't help her and started crying holding my hand.

I really felt very bad hearing her agonizing cry. I consoled her and made her sleep. Since that incident, I'd been very careful in making any comment about her. Similarly, she stopped moving out without informing me. We both mended ourselves to empathise with each other.

'I think you acted very maturely. I'm sure, you shouldn't have any issue after that incident,' said Raj, breaking his silence.

'You can say. I took precaution to ensure all her emotional safety. We opened a joint account and made her to manage all household affairs. Once she was given full responsibility to look after all the family matters, she really became conscious about her conduct. And she ensured that I wasn't hurt by her tantrums.

Our relations really got transformed, when she suddenly got terminally sick. I realised that I'd never given her due respect, what she actually deserved. She'd been managing her work and family so well, I was hardly bothered for anything affecting the family. It was during her illness, I'd to look after my son and other domestic affairs; when I felt how much pain she was taking to look after family without much cribbing. On the contrary, I used to complain for all petty matters. You don't realise the importance of what you've. You come to know the value of things when you don't have it, or when you see it's slipping out of your hand. I got that feeling, when she was critically sick and was struggling for her life. AIMS doctors almost refused to treat her. I couldn't bear an idea to live without her. I prayed day and night and didn't leave any therapy to use for her survival. However, God was really great to bless us. She was back to work after facing six month ordeal of a major surgery, post-operative treatment and tests. Since then we hardly had any issue, which really distressed us.'

'It's really comforting to know that you managed your affairs very well and God blessed you with such a wonderful partner. Please tell me honestly, like I had, you ever have any bitterness on sexual issues? Raj enquired somewhat hesitatingly.

'You're asking a very funny question...'

'No, it isn't a funny. Sex is a vital instrument for cementing emotional relations. It can make or mar a marital relation. You know in my case, it was the sex which actually broke my marriage,' said Raj, interrupting me.

'Yes, I know some cases where the demand for excessive sex led to divorce. People forget that sensual pleasure in marriage isn't one sided and you need to have concern for the wellbeing of your spouse. If she isn't good or not enjoying it for whatever reason, you shouldn't force her. I can share one incident of an army officer, who got married at the age of 31 years with a 20 year old woman. He injured his wife, in his first night, so much so that doctor was called. His wife developed an abhorrence for sex. Whenever he visited home on leave, his wife avoided meeting him fearing unpleasant sex. And finally, she took divorce...'

Interrupting me, Raj said, 'What you say appears reasonable. Marital relations aren't meant just for physical pleasure. I also realised it quite late that husband and wife are the best friends to bond emotionally. One day, I met a middle aged person, who stopped me to get a lift. He asked me to drop him to a hospital located on my way to the office. I gave him a lift. On the way, I asked him, 'Who's admitted to hospital?'

'My wife. I'm supposed to meet her on breakfast at 9.30 a.m. I'm getting late.' He simply answered.

'What's the reason for her hospitalisation?' I further enquired.

'She fell and got injured. And now, she's suffering from loss of memory for last two weeks. She isn't recognising me.' He further informed.

'You said you're to meet her at 9.30 a.m. for breakfast. If she doesn't recognise you, how it matters if you are late?' I questioned him and was stunned by his answer.

'I recognise her, so what if she doesn't. I can't afford to be late and make her wait for the breakfast. All her life she had fed me, and now, how can I neglect her in such a condition, when she needs me the most?' He said with his wet eyes. This incident really moved me.

'It's really a touching story. If I'm obliged to examine marital relations from this perspective, it can be said that marriage not only creates emotional and physical bonding between two different individuals, but it also leads to spiritual harmony, which goes beyond physical unity. It's this union that makes people do anything for each other, even without having physical relation. This emotional or spiritual unity will not touch you, when you've sex out of the marriage...'

'I'm interested to know about your other love tangles, if any, which might've adversely affected your marriage,' Raj further enquired, while interrupting me.

'Everyone knows, extra marital affairs offer momentary pleasure, but do devastate a happy family life and even then people keep on indulging in such relations. I think, it'd been a fixture of human society from its very existence and will remain so till human beings live in this world. I mayn't hesitate in accepting, there'd been some occasions when I got tempted to tread that path, but got saved at the brink. I may share one of such incidents with you. I'd a colleague, who was very lively and humorous. She'd a very respectable place in society and was admired for her sobriety and sincerity. One day, she invited me for dinner and insisted me to come alone without Zoya. Initially, I was reluctant, but on her pestering, agreed and decided to meet her alone in one of the nearby restaurants.

Around 8 p.m., she came to the appointed place. I ordered for a soup. After chatting for some time, I asked her, 'Please tell me the reason for calling me alone.'

'I wanted your advice on my personal affairs. Hope, you won't share this with anyone, including Zoya. Let me confess that I'm not happy with my married life. My husband says if I'm not happy with him, I can have relation with any other person of my choice. What's your suggestion?' She confided me, while posing a serious issue.

I saw a twinkle in her eyes and a mischievous suggestive gesture. I realised what she was hinting to me. It was totally unacceptable. However, without paying any attention to her physical gestures, I commented, 'It's your personal matter, what can I say. I'll appreciate magnanimity, and liberalness of your husband, who can say such a thing. But, I'm not sure, how he may feel if you really act on his advice? No self-respected person can afford to see his wife having extra-marital relations. If you do it, you're going to spoil your family life for all the time to come. As a friend, I'll sincerely advise you to desist from such ideas. I want to see both of you as a happy couple. You mayn't get another doting husband like him, there's no guarantee that you'll be happy with another person…'

Interrupting me, she said, 'You sound like a sermon. I'm really seeking your sincere advice. I mean what I said.'

'I'm also seriously advising you and not just giving you a sermon. I mean what I said to you,' I retorted.

Having sensed my intention from the tenure of my tone, she recoiled and said, 'If it's your honest advice, I'll certainly abide by it.'

'I don't think, you're insane and will do anything which may cause inexorable loss of your reputation and family happiness, just for a momentary pleasure. We mayn't have cordial relations, if you indulge in any unethical conduct,' I said firmly to convey her my point of view.

'I was sure to get a right advice from you. That's why, I wanted to speak to you alone. Please don't tell anything to Zoya, otherwise I won't be able to face her in future,' she said, while apparently feeling obliged. She left promising that she won't do anything wrong.

After some time, I got a message. 'Your advice has increased my respect for you.'

With the passage of time, I gradually distanced myself from that family. There'd been such occasions, when I found myself on a detour. However, I never yielded to any temptations like- 'life is short, have an affair to spice it up.'

'Great. You succeeded in maintaining your chastity. Let me ask you something specific. Didn't you have an issue with Zoya about her sexual behaviour like I had with Teena?' Raj asked me further.

'Raj. I will not rejoice sharing something which should remain buried in the heart of husband and wife. I consider the sexual behaviour of any married person as a sacrosanct affair, which shouldn't be made a subject of public discourse. One shouldn't discuss such personal matters with any friend or relative until some problem is to be addressed. In my view, recourse to sex should be for mutual pleasure and not for unilateral delight. In married life, you should've more concern about your partner's happiness than your own. If you care for your partner's pleasure, you'll be happier. If your partner isn't good and you try to force yourself, you're destined to cause irreparable harm not only to your relations, but also to your partner, whom you claim to love the most....'

Interrupting me, Raj said. 'Jai, I've no intention to know your very intimate moments or feelings. I just wanted to know whether Zoya's conduct ever infuriated you. My experience says there're occasions when your sweetheart is bound to do something mischievous to annoy you. When you're in a very romantic mood and want to make love, she may say I'm on leave. If such pranks are often repeated, they're bound to affect your marital life. I was hinting you such incidents. Don't you think you never encountered such a situation?

'Oh yeah, there'd been several such incidents, you're hinting. She isn't a very romantic partner, who may love anything but sex. Her lack of sensual interest had hardly enthused me to romance with her. Sometimes, her shyness used to really upset me, particularly when there were some special occasions. When I wanted to spend time with her in private, she used to invite friends or relative on such occasions for merry making.

She may spend the whole day with them. Some of her friends may even stay for the night, leaving us no chance for our romantic moments. If someone is at home, she may simply say no. And once she says no, I get annoyed and may not even touch her for weeks. Nevertheless, our sexual relations weren't such determining to knock down our marital card,' I reluctantly shared some of my feelings with Raj.

'I see. You've good married life, despite occasional pitfalls. I think, you're sanguine enough to save your marriage from all oddities. Your compassionate and considerate nature helped you to restore Zoya's confidence in you and regain emotional unity with her. She fulfilled all her commitments, whatsoever, she made with you while marrying you. You succeeded in making a perfect couple, despite your initial doubts about your incompatibility with Zoya. I think, you exhibited remarkable resilience in tackling difficult situations, when you're at the brink of breaking your marriage. Had I acted like you, I might've certainly saved my breakup with Pratibha. Most of the time, we call it our destiny to justify our inhumane, unethical and uncultured egoistic conduct, pretending to champion family pride, religious and social values or what not. Your example proves, what you said earlier, that no one is perfect, but you can make a perfect couple by complementing each other, showing compassion and empathy to your partner. On the contrary, most of us after getting married start finding faults instead of reposing trust in each other. You start suspecting the intentions of your darling, with whom you intended to spend the rest of your life. Alas! Had some good sense prevailed on me, I might've been enjoying today altogether a different life...' Raj commented, while gasping his last words.

'Raj, it's never late. You can still lead your remaining life as a satisfied and happier person than what you'd been so far, if you wish so,' I said.

'Do you think that our age old prejudices against each other can melt down to settle like a molten lava and we can start doting on each other? I can't envisage my wife- Sushma desiring to have a candlelight dinner with me,' Raj said skeptically.

'You shouldn't be pessimistic. I'm sure, she'll be the happiest person in this universe, if you arrange a candlelight dinner to celebrate her next birthday and make it the most memorable day of her life. You should start treating her the way you expect her to treat you. You should spend time with her to build trust and emotional bonding. Being assured of your love, she may jettison her emotional baggage of fear and insecurity to share her hidden and suppressed feelings with you. Once you repose your confidence on her, she may emotionally unite with you, breaking all her barriers. And, she may start behaving in a much sensible way than you ever expected,' I said.

'I tried my best to improve her behaviour, but couldn't help much,' Raj said expressing his disappointment.

'Most of us try to correct our partners, when we see our spouses aren't displaying the traits, qualities, habits, likings or hobbies that we expect from them. Sometime, peer pressure goads us to expect our spouse to copy mannerism of our role model and this expectation becomes a cause of contention to spoil our marital relation. Hence we need to restrain ourselves from too much interference in her lifestyle. The initial years of marriage need more time and efforts to understand each other's nature, likings and disliking. I think, if we manage to show respect and concern to our spouse, chances of having a happy married life may improve…'

Interrupting me Raj said, 'I see merit in your observation. Actually, I tried to force Teena to live in a place, where she never wanted to be. I struggled with Sushma to train her for a lifestyle, she wasn't cut out for. In retrospection, I can say that, perhaps, I committed some serious mistakes which had neither allowed Rita, nor Sushma to have confidence in me. And consequently, we always remained like strangers to each other.'

I saw my watch, it was almost midnight. I asked Raj. 'Let's sleep, it's already 1.45 a.m. We'd been so much engrossed in our discourse that we lost sense of time.'

'Oh yes. We really got lost in sharing our life experiences. I must confess, it was really worth. 'I'll be very happy, if you pen down all that we discussed today. Our deeds and misdeeds may help people, like me, to improve chances of marital happiness. See you tomorrow in the dining hall,' Raj said and left my room.

I closed the door and set an alarm for 7 a.m. before going to bed. It took me some time to sleep. I woke up with the alarm bell ringing, but was feeling too sleepy to wake up, so I switched off the alarm bell. I got up around 8 a.m. in the morning, which was quite late as per my normal routine time of 6 a.m. I got ready and left for breakfast around 9 a.m. Raj and other friends were already there in the dining hall. After exchanging normal morning greetings with friends, I took my plate for filling and sat down on one of the tables, where Raj, Rocky and Sophia were already enjoying their breakfast. Breaking the silence, Rocky asked Raj, pointing towards me, 'What time did you check out from his room? I tried to speak to you around 10 p.m., but there wasn't any response from your room.'

'I was with Jai till 1.45 a.m. We'd a gala time sharing our life time experiences. I must say Jai has a tremendous sense of managing marital relations. I've suggested him to write down all that we deliberated yesterday. It may be a good guide for all those who're really interested in having a happy married life,' Raj said.

'Don't believe him. He's pulling my leg. I've no such expertise to guide people in their marital relations. I just shared what I've experienced in my personal life,' I said.

'I'm not making fun of you. I'm bloody serious. I thought about what you told me yesterday. I'm sure, if you pen down all our experiences, it may certainly help people to manage their family conflicts and lead a peaceful life,' Raj said emphatically.

'There's no harm in considering what Raj is saying? I agree with him. Yesterday, all of us really shared our life time experiences. If the same are collated and penned down systematically, it may certainly have the potential to guide and help people to learn from our commissions and omissions,' Rocky said.

'Jai. No harm, you can consider what these gentlemen are saying. But right now, let's move to the conference room. It's already 10.25 and hardly 5 minutes are left for the program to start,' said Sophia.

We all started moving towards the conference room. Inside the conference room most of the classmates, who could manage to attend this meet, were already present. The conference room was big enough to accommodate about 60 persons. However, we all were just 27 for whom it was big enough to accommodate. It was really shocking to know a few of us were no more and some weren't in a position to attend, despite their desire to meet all of us.

Nagmani was requesting friends to take their seats. It was a rectangular table around which people were seating themselves. At the centre, a beautiful flower vessel was placed to decorate. On every seat a small water bottle, participants list and souvenir were kept. Taking the charge of coordination, Nagmani said loudly, 'I think, most of us have come and now we can proceed. Or should we still wait for a few moments?'

'We can wait for a few minutes. Or, if you're sure that everyone is here, you can start,' said Sophia.

'I think, everyone is here and, if anyone is left, he can join us at any time. It's not a class lecture, if left, he can't cover it,' said Nagmani.

Sophia got up and said, 'Dear Nagmani, at the very outset, let me thank you for convening and organising this get-together at such a beautiful place. It's given us a good opportunity to meet our dear friends after such a long hiatus. Some of us had been in active touch, but we lost touch with most of them. This get-together may revive our old bonding. Yesterday, some of us met in Jai's room and shared our life time experiences. It was a remarkable day, I can't forget it for the rest of my life,' she said and sat down.

'Thanks Sophia. It wouldn't have been possible without every one's cooperation. This place was chosen on behest of Mr Vinayak, who was very keen to celebrate the silver jubilee of our graduation. It's actually Vinayak, who prompted me to organise this meet at this hotel. You all know that this hotel is owned by Vinayak, who's made all logistic arrangements for your comfortable stay in Mussoorie. One day, he told me that he wanted all his friends to join him in this hotel to celebrate the silver jubilee of our graduation. I spoke to some of you, who readily agreed and encouraged me to go ahead. It was a wonderful response, and most of us are here today. On behalf of all of you and on my behalf, I extend my heartiest gratitude to Vinayak.'

The conference room echoed claps and everyone started thanking Vinayak, who got up with folded hands to respond to every one's greetings and said politely, 'I'm privileged to have you all here. You really obliged me to fulfil my dream to see all of you in my hotel to rekindle some of the forgotten joyful moments of our life. I'm sure, you'll take back some new experiences to enliven your life for the rest of the time you're going to live. Once again, I thank you all.' Vinayak sat down after speaking briefly. Everyone complemented Vinayak for his graciousness and the pain he took in organising this event and for extending his hospitality to each one of us.

'You'll be happy to know that our friend Sudhir has written a book on our college history. May I request Vinayak to release this book in commemoration of the silver jubilee of our graduation,' said Nagmani.

The conference room was again filled with loud clapping and appreciation for Sudhir.

Vinayak graciously obliged and released the book, which was circulated among all of us. Every one praised Sudhir for his commendable contribution to make this occasion an eternal remembrance down the lane of memory.

Nagmani got up and suggested, 'May I request all of you to tell us, one by one, about your work, family and place you intend to settle, so that we can be in touch with each other for the rest of our life.'

His suggestion was accepted and participants, one by one, started narrating about themselves. It started with Nagmani, who was next to me on my left and Raj was next to Sophia on my right. Most of the people were brief in telling their past and present work. It was very apparent that old wine wasn't having the warmth of age. Most of them muttered a standard monologue and were reluctant to open their heart; perhaps, life had forced them to distrust people and to elude sharing of their feelings with others. It was Robert, who got up and interrupted to say, 'Why're we so formal? It appears, we're meeting for the first time. Why aren't we exhibiting the spirit which's brought all of us to this distant place? We've taken pains to come here not just for knowing your name and address. I'm sure, this could've been done through WhatsApp. Please be informal and tell us something eventful about yourself to remember you a fresh.'

He exhorted all of us to be informal in sharing feelings, deep rooted in our hearts, as well as some hilarious moments which would excite us. This changed the mood of gathering and people started peeping down their lane of memories. Some told us very interesting stories about their bosses and family, which really enlivened the atmosphere and brought cheerfulness on their faces. Came the turn of Raj, who got up to speak. While thanking to organisers-Nagmani and Vinayak, he vividly described himself and his professional journey. In conclusion, he said, 'I must confess, it's really a hilarious lifetime experience when some of us spoke heart to heart. Yesterday, I discovered my shy friend- Jai has really matured enough to outwit me in personal affairs. I got a lifetime lesson from him. I wish, I should've got it early to put my life on track. Had I attempted to meet him early, perhaps, I might've been much happier person than what I'm today. I request Jai to pen down all that transpired among us yesterday. It may certainly enlighten us, as to how he could find his darling Zoya. And, how did he manage his family affairs to change a devastating situation into a vibrant, happy married life?' He said and sat down.

Sophia, while narrating her story also seconded Raj's view and requested me to share briefly what we all talked about yesterday. Everyone became very curious to know the treasure, we discovered a night before. They all started singing in the same tune- Jai-Jai-Jai, we all're restless to listen to you.

I got up to say, 'Okay, I'll not disappoint you. First of all, I must thank Vinayak and Nagmani for providing us such a wonderful opportunity to meet and exchange our experiences.

Had this alumni meet not taken place, I wouldn't have gotten an opportunity to know what actually tormented my best friend Raj to keep him away from me. I would've vanished into thin air, while cherishing some grudges against him for avoiding me. It was only yesterday, I came to know why he didn't meet me for such a long time. We now feel better and comfortable with each other. It may take a long time to narrate what all we discussed yesterday. However, it can be summed up in saying that all of us, be a boy or girl, start searching for a perfect partner from the time we realise our existence as a male or female. Natural instinct may prompt us to get attracted with the other sex and sometimes we may break all barriers to get united. However, society and families do condition our thinking and make human relations a complex issue. We don't accept the fact that male and female are distinct creation of God, and they see and act differently from each other. When two persons can't be the same, it's fallacious to expect them to think and act uniformly. When we don't appreciate this universal truth, we start finding fault with others. We start correcting others, when we see them behaving and thinking differently. Everyone is right from one's own perception, but suffers infirmities from the other's vantage point. Thus, no one is perfect, but we look for a perfect partner. Men and women are in a perennial quest for a perfect partner, which's a rattling elusive mirage. Our quest for a perfect partner remains an illusion and shadow chasing. Instead of searching a perfect partner, we should humbly accept the innate differences existing between male and female. Couples should try to know their expectations vis-a-vis their strength and weaknesses to complement each other for teaming up. Thus we can certainly make a perfect couple to lead a harmonious and happy married life. If you're compassionate, considerate and respectful to your spouse, it may create an ambience of emotional security. This may make your partner feel confident that she'll be always loved, even if something wrong was done by her before committing to you. She may confide everything to you without having a fear of losing your love and respect. You don't gain anything, if you keep on harping on her past or generalise her conduct on the basis of her past pitfalls. It denies her an opportunity to improve and start a new life. Everyone has the right to get a chance in life. If you don't have that big heart to empathise and forgive, better don't have a relationship, you're bound to doom. Raj confided with me to tell how he couldn't get married with his darling-Pratibha and why he got divorced from his first wife before getting married to Sushma. I shared with Raj my quest for a perfect partner and my tryst with tribulation I had with Zoya, my wife; and how we managed our conflicts to lead a happy life. Every relationship needs some space to grow and constant nurturing to maintain its luster. We'd been no exception. Once again, I thank all of you for taking pain and making this occasion a big success,' I said and sat down.

The conference room was filled with echoes of clapping. Most of them joined Raj in saying, 'Jai we'll look for the day when you're going to gift us with your memoir. It'll be really thrilling to flick through and share them with our better halves, who may really love it. I halted their pestering by promising to fulfil their longing and took leave thanking everyone.

-----------------+----------------------------+---------------------